MEMORY

Victoria Feuerstein

ISBN-10: 1492182028
ISBN-13: 9781492182023
Library of Congress Control Number: 2013917035
CreateSpace Independent Publishing Platform
North Charleston, South Carolina

For Merekat

Come to the edge.
We might fall.
Come to the edge.
It's too high!
COME TO THE EDGE!
And they came,
and we pushed,
And they flew.

Christopher Logue

1

1989
Journal
Buttu Highlands Dig, Uganda

    It laid before us, mesmerizing and miraculous in the jungle silence, every-thing so still as if a sacred battlefield had been unearthed. The bones of hun-dreds of beasts, buried in the forgotten pockets of time, seams worn open, jutted out from the caking mud. Curious the arrangement of the remains, bone upon bone splayed out from the center in one huge concentric spiral, as if one day, the animals had all come together here to wait. Wait for something, someone of great import. I looked over this exhaustive cemetery and sensed anticipation, a promise stolen, the violent swirling and sinking of dashed hope.

    Slowly we secured our way down into the valley. The stratification of the eroded valley walls indicated to me the bones were ancient. The animals had perished in one cataclysmic moment.

    The sun rose above us, and something at the very center of this monstrous circle caught its light. I motioned to the guide to stay behind and with great cau-tion made my way through the exposed bones. I mentally catalogued antelope femur, lion jaw, zebra rib cage, giraffe neck bones, elephant skull. Predator and prey had lain down together. I reached the center and there lay a shiny cylindrical artifact with perplexing glyphs and the most intriguing bones of all—human.

    Francis Chance

2

Present Day
Braddard College, Maine

Francis Chance could not shake the shame he felt. It clung to him like the smell of smoke to charred wood. Rupert Cirrus, dean of Braddard College, hailed him as an archeologist of genius, a seeker of truth. Had Cirrus known the truth, he'd be horrified. Francis was a liar, a thief of the worst kind. He had stolen from his own daughter.

He sagged into his worn leather desk chair, pulled on his bow tie, and let it drop loosely around his collar. It was after midnight. His retirement party had been torture, a slow burn over the flames of self-reproach. Francis ceased the first opportunity to slip away and return to his office. He turned up the desk lamp and looked around his closet-size office. The bookshelves stood empty. Yellowed maps no longer clung to his office walls. In their place were pale, rectangular specters with vacant eyes. Books, their backbones broken, hinges exposed, were stuffed into cardboard boxes pushed together in the far corner of the tiled floor. The boxes yawned open like a clutch of baby birds, mouths wide, hungry, persistent. An ancient tiredness streamed through him.

He pulled a flask of Macallan from his vest pocket, played with the screw top, then placed it on the desk. He dug his hand into his pants pocket and found the small brass key. He had never gone anywhere without it. He took it out, laid it on his desk blotter, and looked down at the small keyhole of the desk drawer. He had locked the artifact away years ago, never opened the drawer since, never confided in anyone. Many times he'd wanted to destroy it, he'd changed his mind a thousand times every day. His daughter didn't know the artifact existed. Didn't know it was meant for her. He felt the familiar stab of regret in his stomach.

The wind outside pushed wet leaves against the office window. They clung there unnaturally, dark silhouettes against the weak glow of a campus streetlight. He watched as one by one, they lost their grip and were sucked away into the darkness. Long ago, well before his daughter Morey's birth, his life had stretched out brightly before him, a young archeologist full of ideas ready to make his mark on the world of archeology. Then the squall of scandal blew shut the doors. Rupert Cirrus, then chair of Braddard's archeology department, was the only man with enough humanity to offer him a job. Even at sleepy Braddard, tucked into the northeast corner of Maine, the talk surfaced.

"Begging your pardon, my dear Dr. Chance," a student half in his cups clumsily pushed his way toward him at a student-faculty tea. "Aren't you the Chance of the Buttu Highland hoax, who pawned off an artifact as genuine? Gentlemen," his voice rose. "Let's toast to Dr. Chance's bloody nerve."

Francis reached for the Macallan, unscrewed the top and took a pull. He felt his right hand tighten around the flask, a vestige of the rage that had raced swiftly down his arm that day and exploded with his best Oxford boxing team right hook square in the student's smug face.

He'd expected to be fired. Rupert negotiated a semester's suspension.

"Off campus," Rupert had barked. He pulled a rental announcement tacked among a million others off the bulletin board of Tunney Hall and handed it to him.

Victorian on Apoquaque Island.
No TV, no phone, secluded.
$50 a month. One renter only.

He remembered his surprise upon first seeing Apoquaque Island rising from the sea like a prehistoric beast, a tower of rocky barren cliffs. The island was a singularity exuding a sense of standing alone against all odds, against time itself.

The Victorian, one hundred years old, maybe older, was too good to be true for the price. It was sturdy, immaculate. Behind it was a barn and tool shed, the grounds ringed by a black pine forest. He settled in with his one bag of clothes, his research, professional journals concerning ancient script and the artifact, ready to prove his condemners wrong. How naïve, how full of hope he had been. How ignorant of the forces that brought him to Apoquaque.

He thought of that late afternoon, that unusually warm Apoquaque day long ago that was still so vivid. He took another swallow of scotch, traced its heat down his throat, felt the expansion of fire in his stomach. He leaned back into his chair, closed his eyes, and allowed the memories life.

A storm birthed and crackled above the island. Francis stepped out of the Victorian to look. Wind pulsed around him and the air felt liquid, alive. He felt oddly excited. Black and gray thunderheads swollen with rain contorted and electricity jumped from one to another. Thunder rolled across a huge sky as if searching for something.

The entire sky seemed to drop and close around the Victorian's grounds, like a pot lid keeping things contained, brewing, giving him the feeling that if he were just a bit taller, he could reach into the cloud cover swelling above him, touch it, feel it, commune with this writhing-in, bellowing-out force. Eerily beautiful, its energy drew him. He felt he needed only to surrender to be carried up.

The first rain hissed down in small aqua pebbles. Then it hit. The first clap of thunder so loud he felt a push against his eardrums. The electricity of primitive instinct shot down his legs and sent him running toward the tool shed. Drenched, he burst through the double shed doors. A white flash blinded him and instantaneously an angry roar bellowed through the shed. He looked around at his shelter - rusty nails, cobwebs, wood mildewed, softened by the elements - and wondered if he'd made a smart choice. Then a blast of white light and a gunshot of thunder drew his attention back to the open doorway and the furious demon outside.

Water spilled from the sky in strange swells like the ebb and flow of the ocean's surf or the metered opening and closing of an ancient door - too heavy a downpour to see one moment, a clear view the next.

That's when it happened.

Looking out, Francis realized something else was out there. Something stood in the liquid downpour, something dark not more than thirty feet from the shed, its eyes looking into his.

He took a step back into the shed and the figure moved equally closer. A chill shot up his spine. He strained to make out the image but the rain-door banged shut with a thunderclap and he could see nothing through the curtain of water. He felt a queer sense of being stalked. The words *open the door* screamed in his mind.

As if obeying his command, the rain subsided and his vision cleared. He stood immobilized looking straight at a thoroughly soaked woman. Tall, slender, sinewy, yet absolutely feminine, she was a miracle. Their gazes locked and he fell into the dark pools of her eyes.

Fear dissolved into amazement.

The woman smiled. A gorgeous smile.

He moved aside.

With the grace of a cat, she moved in out of the storm and stood next to him. He felt awkward, alien in his lanky body. She said nothing just stared out into the rain. He reached for an old blanket from a nearby crate and pulled it free. As he drew nearer to her, her scent - earthy, enticing - filled him. He placed the blanket around her slender shoulders fearful she might vanish as mysteriously as she had appeared. He turned and watched the rain.

He did not know how long this moment lasted. Time seemed to defy earthly laws. And when she turned her face to his, he did not meet her gaze. He knew her dark penetrating eyes were studying him, knew even then, that first day, he must avoid them.

Francis opened his eyes. As always the memory left him agitated. He brought his hands to his head, ran his fingers through his hair, squeezed hard, felt the anger that belonged singularly to betrayal. She had seduced him, used her magic to get what she wanted - the artifact and a daughter. But he had won. He had taken both from her. He had no choice. He had to protect his daughter, Morey. Wasn't that what the thievery, the lies were about? His mouth felt dry with the ashes of self-deceit.

He thought of their Morey, now grown, stunning. She had her mother's exotic beauty, her mother's dark, mesmerizing eyes. And she had her mother's magic. The magic that once flowed through her mother's veins pulsed through Morey's, he was sure of it. Magic perhaps diluted by his union with her mother but magic nonetheless. Magic his only child did not know was hers.

He reached for the small brass key, fingered it. His hand trembled slightly. He felt too weary to continue the fight. Secure walls of time shielded him from Morey's mother yet she haunted him nonetheless. Long ago, she stole into his subconscious, pushed into his dreams, and now, like the Apoquaque storm, the dream was gathering strength. He awakened most mornings exhausted, the dream the first thing on his mind.

Morey's mother stood in front of him. Her gaze fell to the artifact he held in his hand. She said nothing but he knew she wanted the artifact back. It belonged to their daughter.

The truth shall set you free, he reflected.

A gust of wind rattled the window, pushed chilled wet air through the brittle pane.

Francis took in a deep breath, let it out. The vapors of alcohol fogged around him. He wished he were braver than he was. He wished he hadn't lied to his daughter. He reached for the key, placed it in the keyhole, turned it, and felt the bolt give. It was time to rectify things.

He opened the drawer and looked inside.

"The stuff of the heavens," he said softly.

3

Botswana, Africa

She remembered. Last night as she stood outside her tent, she'd heard her name spoken aloud.

Morey. So close, breath prickled the nape of her neck. So distinct, she'd swung around. No one was there.

The morning's orangey glow did not warm the untidy edges of her sanity. She looked out over the African savanna and shivered. Her twenty-fifth birthday had come and gone. For weeks, an anticipatory sensation had thrummed in her chest, told her something big was going to happen. Something did happen. But it wasn't welcome; it wasn't good. A crack had formed in her world and let the dream out. Her childhood dream, once submerged in the netherworld of her sub-conscious, had awaken from its muddy slumber and like an amphibian peering out from the edges of the bog, it debated whether this margin was the beginning or the end, slip too close to the brink, spill over and become something else, someone else whose memory may not include its old markers. The thought shook her to the core. And now last night's disembodied voice. What was happening?

She needed to shake off the edginess she felt, put her mind to the day's plans. She zipped up her jacket and looked toward camp. Wekesa was stoking the fire, preparing breakfast. The smell of pork-and-fennel sausage wafted toward her. She felt the hunger in her stomach but decided this indulgence must wait. She had work to do. She tugged at the leather strap slung around her neck to equalize the weight of her camera and thought of the *National Geographic* deadline she'd already missed by two weeks. She pushed through her inertia and started down the hill.

Daniel Gunther leaned on her Land Rover, his Pentax LX resting against his chest. A quizzical look stole over his face when he saw her coming.

"Morey Chance?"

"Expecting someone else?" She glared at him.

"No, sorry. I thought—"

"Memory Chance. Short form – Morey," she shook her head, weary of the persistent presumption of maleness that came with her name and her profession, wildlife photographer. She swung herself into the Land Rover, started it up and waited for him to move.

"Which way you heading today?" Daniel's hand rested on the passenger door.

"Northeast, past Savuti camp," she released the brake.

"Won't find them there."

"Oh really?" she shot him a look.

"She's moving her cubs. They're hungry. Today she'll make her kill." His eyes studied her.

"You've seen them?" Her voice lifted. She had tracked the lioness for days, found the remains of a large wildebeest eaten down to bones hidden under a fig tree. The lioness and her four cubs however continued to elude her. "Where?" she asked then caught the hopeful look in his eyes and immediately regretted it.

He removed the camera's strap from his neck, turned the camera around and held it out for her to see his shot.

Her gaze dropped to his camera. Daniel's image of the lioness shielding her cubs against a male lion had as its focal point the fixed stare-down of the mother. It was almost impossible to look away from that maternal glare of protectiveness. It was one of those pictures that stopped people dead in their tracks.

"You have talent." She heard the softening in her voice. *Don't,* she reminded herself. She looked hard at him: tall, sandy hair, rangy - almost scrawny - probably in his early twenties.

"Ten frames per second." His voice lifted. "One-third stop increments in shutter speed and aperture, the quietest for working in the field."

"I have a rule," she said flatly. "I never break it."

"I don't believe what they say about you." His words came out rushed. He looked surprised by them. "Silly superstition, that's all." His voice trailed off.

Her face felt hot. "Maybe you should," she snapped.

He looked confused, opened his mouth as if to speak but no words came out.

"Look, believe this curse stuff, don't believe it. I don't care. Rule is I do my shoots alone. No exceptions. That includes you."

He looked wounded. He turned his camera around and looked at the shot. "She's beautiful. What a mother raising four fat cubs. Good luck." He turned to go.

Her fingers played agitatedly on the steering wheel. *National Geographic* would soon be getting impatient. And Daniel was not going to give up the lioness's whereabouts. Not unless he went along.

"Hold it," she said.

He turned back, flashed his smile. "Let me ride with you, watch what you do." His voice edgy with excitement, he moved toward the Land Rover like a kid being called off the bench to bat. "Your work captures the wild heart. I want to learn from you. I'll stay out of your way."

She stared into the sapphire of his South African eyes, tried to read if he would survive. *Survive.* The flat wall of reality hit her. What was she thinking? There was no room for speculating. She turned her face away from him, looked straight ahead through the windshield, and steeled herself.

"I'm sorry." She reached for the gearshift, shifted into first, pushed her foot down hard on the accelerator. The Land Rover lurched forward, tires spitting stones, pushing up a dust cloud. She glanced in the rearview mirror. Daniel stood in her wake.

She rode for over an hour before she let the Land Rover roll to a stop. Ahead of her the land dropped sharply to a plain that went on seemingly forever. Something in Daniel's photo had caught her eye. An orangey-red smear of mud on the lioness's left foreleg. She looked down the escarpment to a stream that cut through the copper-colored earth below. On the other side tall grasses stretched south. More than a hundred water buffalo drank from the lip of the steam, hooves caked orange-red. Every few moments, the beasts raised their heads nervously, listening. They sensed something watching, waiting in the grass.

The morning sun was still low in the sky when she saw them - white tips of ears camouflaged in the reeds. Morey grabbed her camera, set it on tracking mode. Quietly she climbed from the Land Rover and made her way down the steep ledge. In front of her were a hundred spooked water buffalo, behind her the fifteen-foot wall of the escarpment. Not a safe place. But the light and the angle were perfect. Through the reeds, she could make out the lioness, stone-still. Closer. She glanced up to her Land Rover and instantly felt something drop in her stomach. A second Land Rover behind hers, empty. She knew it was Daniel's. He'd not taken no for an answer. Where was he?

A water buffalo bolted from the water, sent a shudder of movement through the herd. Ears twitching, two large males watched the grass for movement then ventured back into the shallow water, lowering their heads to drink. Morey felt the danger in her own body - a skipped heartbeat, a low-key tremor in her consciousness.

Go back. Find Daniel.

Then she saw the yellow eyes, the massive muscles quivering with adrenaline, the lioness at the edge of the wall of grass. Morey took a deep breath, steadied herself, and raised her camera.

The click she heard was not the click of her camera but of Daniel's somewhere behind her. Instantly came the sound of the lioness crashing through the grass, the spray of water glistening in the air, the frantic bleating of captured prey. The water buffalo panicked. Sad long faces and wild cow eyes, obscured in a cloud of dust and spray, surged toward Morey. The heaving, shoving throng surrounded her. The thunder of their hooves and their wild bellowing were deafening.

Morey did not have to look behind her to know the moment Daniel was gone.

The tawny lioness pulled her victim from the stream, disappeared with it into the grasses. Morey heard the mewing of the cubs. She looked back to where Daniel's body lay like a bag of rags, pummeled by hundreds of panicked hooves. The settling dust caught the light, and the silence grew surreal. Her gaze dropped to the ground at her feet, the earth carved, gorged everywhere - everywhere except for the untouched intact circle in which she stood.

Not one water buffalo had touched her.

Morey.

She heard her name and knew. There was no escaping this whisper, entreating her to leave what she knew as solid, safe and enter some enormous space where something else was breathing the truth of her.

4

Morey stood at the back of the church, her eyes bleary from fatigue. Sleep eluded her. A thousand drums pounded behind her temples. She stared at Daniel's closed coffin, his small family standing vigil by its side. She watched his mother's shoulders rise and fall in soft sobs, his sister wrapped in her father's arms. Death had crashed into their world and crushed them.

Morey caught the look on his sister's face and watched her body go rigid when she saw her.

"How dare she." The sister's words cut the air.

Mourners turned to look eyes widened in surprise and a rumbling of hushed words flowed around Morey like a toxic cloud.

The father's face contorted with pain, anger. He did not speak but his message was clear. *You have robbed us.*

"Get out." The words croaked from the sister's throat.

Morey stood, silent, awkward. She opened her mouth to say the words: *I'm sorry, so very sorry.* Nothing came out.

"Get out, heks! Get out!" the sister screamed.

Morey pushed open the church door and half-stumbled into bright African sunlight that stung her eyes like needles. Light-headed, her legs unsteady, her mind spinning, she stopped for a moment to steady herself at the top of the church steps.

"What the hell was that about?"

Morey turned and looked into small dark eyes set closely in a round face shadowed with stubble. Edgar Maier, assistant editor of *National Geographic*, the guy who had landed her this assignment. Edgar was to her what theater people call their "angel." He'd seen a special quality in her work and believed in her talent. Once she'd overheard him on the phone promoting an assignment.

"Morey Chance goes out on shoots like a wild animal, ready for the unexpected. And bam, she nails it. You look at her photo and the animal seems closer to you than your own skin. It seems like you become the animal looking out of the shot. Crap, the hair goes up on your neck."

She remembered the heady rush she felt then listening to Edgar compliment her work. She was surprised by the feeling, the depth and pleasure of it, this feeling of being understood. She looked at him now and saw worry, that confidence in her gone. She accepted why he would regard her with new concern and even a measure of wariness.

"What's this heks stuff?" he said.

"Heks," she repeated her voice flat, empty. "It's Afrikaans for witch."

"They're calling you a witch?"

"Pretty much, what would you think? A herd of water buffalo crushes Daniel and miraculously leaves me standing completely untouched?"

"I'd say you're damn lucky."

"Lucky? You know this is not the first time." Her words came fast, angry.

"Accidents," he turned his face from her, looked down at his feet. "Accidents happen, Morey." His tone, low and sad betrayed him. He knew, like her, something was seriously wrong.

"I heard something, Edgar."

He looked at her.

"I heard my name. After Daniel—"

"Don't." He cut her off. "The guy yelled out your name before—" Edgar stopped himself.

She was silent. Wonderful, generous Edgar wanted to keep the sinking ship afloat. A year ago when the first life was lost, there was no denying it had been her mistake. It was her foot that slipped letting the Sumatran tiger know they were there. But the beast tore past her as if she didn't exist and took her partner down. Then there was

Zimbabwe, the bull elephant that side-stepped her but badly injured her guide. Still, she wanted so badly to believe Edgar's accident theory that she almost did, until now.

She'd created her rule. She'd do her shoots alone. No exceptions. Then she started pushing the margins, started getting in close, closer than she'd dared before, foolishly close. It wasn't about some crazy death wish, some adrenalin rush. A different hook kept her pushing the envelope. It was that feeling, that feeling of being alive, 100 percent living, breathing, heart-pounding alive. She'd never noticed its absence from her life till she experienced it. She never felt it more acutely than when she was a breath away from a wild animal. Being labeled a witch did not matter. All that mattered was this feeling she could no longer live without.

"Listen, *National Geographic* is pulling the plug." Edgar was all business now. "It's not that they're blaming you for what happened." She heard the lie in his voice. "Publishing pictures after a death doesn't go over well with readers. The assignment's been scrapped."

She didn't care. She turned away from him and looked out at the church parking lot. "I should have turned back." She felt a lump rise in her throat. "Daniel had talent. You should have seen his work. When he wasn't in his Land Rover, I should have—" She fought back tears. She hadn't cried since childhood. She was angry with herself for this weakness, loath to cry in front of Edgar Maier on these church steps in broad daylight.

"Best you get out of Botswana especially with this witch crap. Lay low. Do some freelance work." He let his hand rest briefly on her shoulder. "I'll call you in a few months, when things get back to normal."

She watched him walk down the church steps to his dusty blue Avis Escort. He turned back to her, threw her a wave, got in, and drove off. She knew what Edgar didn't. Things would never be normal again. Whatever rocked and swayed below her conscious mind's surface was rising, on the verge of flooding into the present.

The night of her twenty-fifth birthday her childhood dream had breached the levy walls. That overwhelming inescapable dream was back, closer, hungrier, palpably real, and her nice, tight sense of reality was unraveling. For Daniel, for herself, she would not run any longer.

5

Hill leaned back from the heat of the campfire into the canvas camp chair, her stomach still warm from a bowl of maize-meal porridge. She gazed at the Land Rover caked thick with saffron dust, parked at the tent she shared with her guide, Mbokwe. For months they had traveled the bush together, studying the white rhinoceros. The tent caught the light of the campfire and beyond the rolled-up canvas door, the tangled muddle that was her sleeping bag, socks, and knapsack was visible.

Mbokwe poked a stick into the fire. A flutter of sparks rose then extinguished one after the other save one that swayed upward into the dark. Hill followed the tiny glowing cinder until it was indistinguishable among the million stars of the Milky Way and thought of it drifting endlessly in the vast vacuum of stellar space unbridled by the gravity of responsibility. The thought was freeing and somehow relieving. She reached inside her vest pocket and pulled out an oblong leather pouch closed by a pull-string. She loosened the string and slid the cylindrical artifact into her hand. Its touch used to light her with a fullness brought forth from the knowledge of the goodness that would be accomplished by the artifact's powers. Now she felt as though the cylinder might pass through the skin, veins, and bones of her hand as if she were a ghost made up of the white ashes of loss.

Mbokwe looked over at the cylinder. "Ah, very old," he said respectfully.

"Yes, my friend. Ancient."

Mbokwe nodded. "Anchor's?"

Hill felt her stomach tighten. "No. This one belongs to me."

Mbokwe looked seriously into the fire as if he sensed his question crossed some emotional line. "Tonight we go to Bushmen's camp?" Mbokwe asked.

"Tonight," she answered.

"Get ready then." Though Bantu, Mbokwe's Bushman heritage was evident in his small stature, yellowish dark skin and lack of ear lobes. He stood and kicked out the fire.

Hill slipped the cylinder back into the pouch and returned it to her vest pocket. She stood and looked out over the endless ocean of dry land and grasses. The one good thing about the Kalahari Desert was that you could see someone coming. She walked over to the Land Rover, swung herself into the driver's seat and started her up. She pulled the Land Rover over to the dying campfire and waited for the jostle that meant Mbokwe was in the back.

After a half hour of bumping through dried land Hill made out firelight in the distance. On previous visits the Bushmen had lit two fires. The second smaller fire signaled she and Mbokwe were welcome. Should there be only one fire, she must turn around and go back to the camp.

A bushbuck caught in their headlights looped into higher grass. Hill slowed the Land Rover.

"One fire, just one," Mbokwe said, his voice tight.

Hill cut the engine. The Land Rover rolled to a stop. From here she could see the Bushmen leader circling the campfire in a dance to call the spirits. His movements were mimicked by two other men, one of whom Hill knew to be the leader's son. Five women sat outside the dance chanting. The rest of their small community grouped together in front of their huts, watching intently, swaying to the leader's rhythm.

"I do not know this dance. I do not know this song." Mbokwe sounded wary, almost frightened. "Different, very different."

Hill listened to the chanting voices. The rhythmic shuffling of the men's feet and the flames licking the cool night air were hypnotic. Her friend was right. There was something different going on here. She looked up into the clear African night and knew what Mbokwe didn't. Tonight the sky would change, bleed a different color.

"We must go," Mbokwe insisted.

Hill started up the Land Rover and turned it around, kicking up a funnel of dust. She looked back through the dusty film and watched the dancers' shadowy ritual. The Bushmen knew it was coming. Hill knew as well. She knew also that when it was over the white rhinoceros would be gone from Africa.

6

British Columbia, Canada

"We had an agreement."

Her father's voice, distant and harsh, scratched at her mind. She slipped her lanky girl legs from the covers and went to the door. The sharp sound of her father's heels hitting the kitchen floorboards, back and forth as far as the telephone wire reached, rang up the stairwell, pounded in her brain.

"You broke your promise. Now I must protect her." His tone was unforgiving, his voice determined.

She looked at the red glow of her alarm clock. Whom was he talking to at two in the morning?

"No. Not on her eleventh birthday. Not on any birthday."

He was talking about her. Heart pounding, she strained to hear.

"She has the magic." She heard a woman's voice. Impossible, yet she did.

"Magic," he said the word as if it were poison. "It's too dangerous. I won't permit it." The sound of his footfalls stopped where the telephone cradle hung on the kitchen wall. "Don't you understand?" His voice grew sharper. "It's ended. I don't care what powers you believe she has. I meant what I said. Contact me again, come anywhere near Morey, I'll expose you. All of you." The sharp sound of the receiver slamming into the cradle echoed through the house.

Her hands flew to her ears.

Morey woke from her dream the way she always did, pulse racing, the roar of her bloodstream thudding in her ears, the familiar edge of claustrophobia. Her hands white-knuckled the copilot seat of the Piper Seneca.

"Didn't mean to wake you," the pilot had reached over to pick up the empty Coke can resting at the heel of her left foot.

She put her hand on his shoulder, stopping him.

"Can just slipped out of my hand." A crooked grin tugged at Claude Taub's mouth, hung there like a question mark. He shrugged. His small brown eyes, visible between the ragged brim of his faded baseball cap and navigator sunglasses, were rimmed in red. His leather jacket was open over his bulging chest and stomach, the leather of the right arm shredded as if raked by a Maine Coon cat.

She said nothing, bent down, picked up the can, and tossed it over her shoulder into the fuselage of the two-seater. The can hit the metal floor behind her with a clang and rolled to a stop.

Claude apparently got the message. He straightened in his seat. "What brings a pretty girl like you flying into the remotest part of British Columbia?"

"A test," she put her fingers to her temples, applied pressure. It sometimes helped.

"Test," he half-laughed, exposing cigarette-stained teeth. "Well, you'll get one. Nobody's been to this camp in God knows how long. No telling what you'll find."

"Crazy, huh?" She let her hands drop to her lap, half-smiled at the word she was beginning to think defined her. In her mind, she saw an image of herself slowing rocking in a dark corner of an asylum's ward, arms wrapped tightly, hugging her legs to her chest.

"Crazy. Yeah, I'd say. And I'm probably the only pilot crazy enough to take you there."

He was right. She'd tried and no one else would pilot her there. Morey shifted in her seat. She hated the close quarters of bush planes, the cold air leaking into the cabin, the noise reverberating in her ears.

"Don't even know if we'll be able to land." Claude stretched to look out the front window. "Been so long, the field could be overgrown."

Through her window she saw the dark green of the forest give way to a patch of open land. A square dot of brown marked the roof of a cabin. Her anxiety lifted; her pulse calmed. She felt the way she usually felt minutes after waking from the dream, incomplete, empty. An emptiness that hurt.

The dream had begun years ago, the night of her eleventh birthday. Then it left her feeling as if she were waiting for something to happen that would take a very long time to come but that one day she would understand everything. The hope that the turned page might yield some kind of foothold of an explanation, the next clue, the translation to this dream she didn't understand. That day never came. Since Daniel's death the dream inhabited every sleeping moment. When she woke the emptiness she felt left her driven, hungry, as obsessed with the dream as it seemed to be with her.

Claude dropped the Piper's airspeed and the penetrating drone of the engines softened.

"Sure you don't want to change your mind?" Claude said.

"Thanks, I'm sure."

"Suit yourself." He pushed the half-wheel and the plane dropped into its descent.

The ground came up fast. Morey sized up the length of the field and thought it way too short. The plane hit the ground, bounced twice, jolted along the grass strip heading straight for a dense wall of trees. She braced herself. The Piper went to the tree wall and stopped, nose resting scant feet from dense black spruce saplings.

"Now that's what I call a landing. Good girl, Millie." Claude patted the instrument panel and turned the engine off. He looked out the front window. "Forest's sure swallowed up this strip, mighty hungry these Canadian woods," he sly-eyed Morey. "Time to unload your gear, then we'll need to turn Millie around."

Morey was more than happy to plant her feet on *terra firma*. She opened her door and swung herself out. Dust from the landing rose up her nose - goldenrod pollen and dirt. Humpbacked mountains dominated by lodgepole pine encircled the strip. No wind. Silence filled the air, the sound of the forest watching them.

The one-room cabin stood twenty yards from the plane. It looked tired and worn. Its frame listed slightly to the north as if the cruel winter winds had buffeted it off its foundation. The thought crossed her mind that the cabin would be happier if allowed to lie down. She heard the pilot's heavy steps approaching the tail and decided to open the fuselage door herself. She did not want his help. The door slid easily. She reached in for her backpack, swung its strap over her left shoulder, and grabbed a rolled sleeping bag and the cardboard carton she had secured with rope.

By the time he rounded the tail she had deposited her gear a short distance from the plane. "Ready to turn her around," she said.

Claude looked at her scant gear, at her, like she was some exotic animal. "Right," he studied her. "Anyway," he tilted his head to the sky, "got to get going before the light goes."

She took the right wing and he took the left. The plane rolled back easily. They turned it until the nose pointed back down the strip.

"Last chance, Morey Chance." Claude laughed, apparently amused by his little rhyme.

"See you in two weeks," she said flatly. A thought flashed through her mind. "You won't forget me?" She stared into his opaque sunglasses.

"Cross my heart." He made the motion, pushed his sunglasses down his nose, and gave her a wink.

She watched as Claude hoisted his weight into the pilot's seat, shaking his head, likely thinking she'd soon be bear meat.

"Keep your eyes peeled for Sasquatch." He closed the pilot's door. She couldn't wait for him to leave.

The plane taxied off and rose up over the trees like a feather. She watched until she no longer heard the Piper's engines nor saw anything but a silver glint in the sky. Before she gathered her gear she looked into the dark curtain of trees and wondered if anything was looking back.

The cabin held no surprises. It was an empty shell devoid of furniture, cobwebs hanging from every imaginable place. Spiders, an assortment of insects and rodents had laid claim to the structure years before. Droppings covered much of the floor. She cut a leafy branch from a chokeberry bush outside the cabin and used it to sweep the floor clean. She unrolled the sleeping bag then she stepped back outside and stood looking at the sky.

Twilight was different in the mountains. It faded to black so quickly the shift was palpable, yet there was a window in time, ever so brief, just before the light left when the air glowed. When the light of day mingled with the light of night, a rich time when dreams and reality intermingle and share a brief kiss - a magical time that made her feel part of something larger, something sacred.

That was why she was here, to find the Sacred Valley, if it existed at all. She remembered the Northwest Indian lecture series, the soft, raspy voice of Chief Light Paw weaving the story of the Sacred Valley of the Bears. The legend told of the white man coming, his attitude that bears were dangerous vermin to be eradicated as if they were a disease. The bears called upon the mountains to protect them, to close around them and form a secret valley - a sacred valley only beasts and brethren could enter.

The story had touched a chord in Morey. Long after the lecture, it thrummed in her subconscious, pushed her until she began hunting for more information. Tidbits related in the slightest way to the legend - trappers' reports dating from the 1800s, lost backpackers' wild stories, even pilots' tales - all she examined, catalogued. Now she would use it for her test. There was no Daniels here to be maimed or killed. She was alone.

Night fell. An ink-black sky filled with cold sparkling stars. Morey built a small fire a safe distance from the cabin and heated a pan of pork and beans. There was something comforting about pork and beans and a campfire. She crouched low by the fire's glowing embers and wondered if her plan was insane or if she was.

She would leave the carton containing cooking gear at the cabin. The small quantities of freeze-dried food, enough to make it through two weeks and two extra days just in case, she transferred to her backpack. The backpack was already loaded with a canteen, a hooded rain slicker, a thin blanket, a flare, her Canon, a first-aid kit, a wool hat, a Swiss-army knife, a compass and a rope to suspend the backpack between trees far enough apart and high enough that a bear couldn't reach it.

"A bear's nose is so good he can smell your track when it's three days old and figure out the color of your mother's wedding dress,"

Claude had said back in Vancouver just after she had laid five crisp hundred-dollar bills into his hand.

Morey had studied bear behavior, and she was a fanatic about a clean camp. She'd read about one bear attack where the bear had taken a two-hundred-pound man in its mouth and shaken him, leaving scuffmarks in the dirt. She knew that what a bear wanted most was to be left alone. Do not surprise a bear. Never look a bear in the eyes.

Morey took one last look at the forest. Even with the stars out, its blackness was solid. It seemed closer than before. She knew people who would be unnerved by being alone in the dark wilderness, spooked even but for her nature was nectar, sustenance for the soul, a connection to something more real, more meaningful than anything found amongst the shoving, breath-sucking masses of humanity.

She checked the fire and decided it was safe to let it die out. Its faint light was good company. With the backpacking that was ahead of her, she needed the rest of a peaceful night's sleep. She prayed she would not dream tonight - not that dream anyway, so real each time when she awoke she expected to be standing at her bedroom door in that old house with her father downstairs, the fine line between dream state and consciousness melted. So real she was beginning to wonder if it had been a dream at all.

Exhausted, she slipped into the sleeping bag and hoped sleep would come easily. A part of her wondered if this search was a mistake. If this would be the time she died.

7

Braddard College

"Professor Chance?"

Francis Chance looked up from his desk. He hadn't heard his office door open.

"Excuse me, *Dr.* Chance." The man tilted his head toward the block letters - Francis Chance, PhD, Archeology Department - on the door. Francis wasn't sure, but he thought he heard sarcasm.

"I am Dr. Chance." The man's appearance startled Francis. Ramrod straight, short military haircut, immaculate business suit, definitely not standard, laid-back Braddard College attire. "And you are?"

"John Feuer." He reached inside his jacket, pulled out a thin leather wallet, and flashed an ID. "National Security Agency."

"NSA, I don't understand." There was something about this guy Francis didn't like.

Feuer entered the closet-size office, glanced at the empty bookshelves and stacked cardboard boxes. "Are you going somewhere, Doctor?"

Suddenly Francis had the queer feeling Feuer had been here, looked around his office before. He didn't like him, didn't like him at all. He wished he were younger, stronger.

Francis ignored his question. "What is it that you want?"

"I'm interested in your thesis. The one based on the Buttu Highland's dig."

"My thesis?" he felt the hairs on his neck stand up. He'd written it years ago for Morey's mother's eyes only. Proof he'd meant business, would expose them if they came for Morey. "That's centuries old." He tried to sound dismissive. "I wrote it when I was a much younger man full of ideas not rooted in solid research." He swallowed hard, then he remembered. "That was never published. How did you—"

"You never mentioned the artifact in your thesis."

"Artifact?" his eyes flickered to the desk drawer.

"A cylinder with hieroglyphics," Feuer's gaze followed his.

"The article you described was discredited." Frances sensed this man knew that full well.

"And a talented young Oxford-educated archeologist, a bright rising star, was accused of the worst sin in the archeological world - a hoax."

Francis stiffened, stood. He did not want to be talking to this man, did not want to be alone with him in his cramped office.

"That was a long time ago and I'm sure you can understand why I'd rather not remember that time of my life. Besides, I have a class to teach. You'll have to excuse me."

Feuer just stood there. Then Francis detected a slight pull at the corner of the man's mouth, a smirk. Francis felt it clearly then, pure menace.

"Perhaps you didn't hear me," Francis said. He heard the sound of talking behind Feuer, students in the hallway. Feuer's head turned slightly. He'd heard them too.

"Another time," Feuer's crooked lip grew to a smile. "Soon," he turned and left the office.

Francis collapsed into his chair. He had not shown his thesis to anyone. And the artifact. God, what was happening? He thought of his daughter, Morey, grabbed the phone and punched in her number.

Three rings and her answering machine picked up.

"Sorry, off on a photo expedition. Please leave a message."

He decided not to leave a message. He had to think this through. Besides, he hadn't spoken to his daughter in months. God, was it over a year?

Two framed pictures sat on his desk, the last things he'd left unpacked. He leaned in and gazed at one. Morey, barely five then, so innocent, so vulnerable, sat with her arms draped around his neck. He felt that familiar pang in his stomach, the feeling he had failed her. He shifted his gaze to the other photograph. A deep gash cut into the mahogany frame, its glass long absent, shattered the day he flung it against the corner of the bookshelf. Tall, fit, bright blue eyes grinning, a much younger Francis stood beside a striking woman. Her beautiful face captured him. Dark eyes, black shining pools that seemed at the same time infinitely deep and supernaturally piercing still drew him in.

He ran his thumb along the side of the frame, rested it on the gash, pushed his flesh into its wound.

There were moments when the turn of a corner made all the difference. What would his life have been like had he not followed the guide into the rainforest, never found the cylindrical artifact? He was convinced if not for the artifact, he'd never have traveled to Apoquaque, never have met the wonderful being who was to become Morey's mother.

He looked at the wall clock. His last class. He had to get to class then he'd figure out what to do. He placed his hands on his desk, leaned in and pushed himself to his feet. The glass cover of his daughter's photograph caught his reflection. His face looked gray, old. Something in him was tired. Exhausted.

He eased the photographs into his valise. Closing the lid, he watched its shadow darken the contents. He pressed the two locks, listening to the cold metal clicks as if they meant something. He walked to his office door and without looking back closed it behind him. He made his way down the corridor.

Vito, the custodian, was on his knees banging on an ancient radiator with a wrench. A familiar scene. He lifted his head and smiled, "Hi, Doc."

Francis nodded.

"You OK, Doc? You look—"

"I'm fine, Vito. Just a little tired."

Francis felt Vito's gaze follow his slow walk to the glass doors, through the doorway and out of Tunney Hall.

He was halfway cross the grass commons when he looked up and saw Feuer walking straight at him.

"Hey!"

Feuer crashed into him almost knocking him down. Francis felt a hot pinprick at his neck and turned. Feuer kept walking. An intense heat spread down Francis's neck, settled against his chest, pushing, making it difficult to breathe.

He sensed his body tumble, felt cool damp grass at the back of his head. Shadow people gathered over him in an indecipherable pattern shot through with shafts of azure sky. He sensed speech, heard nothing. He thought of Morey and became filled with anxiety. *She must know! She has to be told!* How unfair of him to deny her. How foolish of him to try and stop it. It was he who had been afraid. Then he remembered. Feuer was too late. The cylinder. Thank God he had sent it. The cylinder would lead her.

Magic. What form would it take?

He felt a slight smile. It was the only part of his body he could feel.

8

Morey rose before dawn, rubbed her eyes, tried to focus. The dream had continued its invasion of her nights. She awoke tired, afraid she was losing her edge. It was her seventh day backpacking and at this elevation the nights were cold, the mornings chilly. She munched on a granola bar with blueberries. Her breath condensed into small clouds with each bite. The sun rose filtering yellow light through the trees, warming the air. She took off her wool cap and stuffed it into her backpack, rubbed her fingers vigorously through her matted short hair, and stretched. Today was her last day. If she did not head down the mountain tomorrow she'd risk not being back in time to meet Claude. She'd seen black-tailed deer, porcupine, moose, marmots, bats, owls, eagles; she'd found overturned rocks, diggings, old bear claw marks scratched into Douglas fir, the ground around them littered with decaying wood chips, all signs this was bear territory. But no bear.

To secure a fresh supply of water, she'd followed a creek into the mountains. The forest was thick with lodgepole pine and Engleman spruce, saplings edged close to the stream's lip. Visibility was less than twenty feet. She knelt down by the creek bed to refill her canteen and placed her hand smack in the middle of it - a bear print in the soft creek mud. It clearly showed the five toes and the five points where the claws entered. Huge, twice the width of her head, the bear had to be nine hundred, one thousand pounds. She looked closely. The print was fresh.

Morey scanned the trees, saw nothing. A noise drew her to a patch of timber so thick it eclipsed the light. She heard it - the sound of breathing, huge lungs pumping gently. Close. She crouched, stilled. Through the thickness she found his small brown eyes. As big as a horse with a shaggy coat of silvery brown fur, he stared back at her.

Grizzly.

The bear gave her the most intense stare she had ever received from any living thing. Time seemed to stop. She should have dropped her gaze, but did not, would not. This was the test she wanted. She waited for the bear to make his move. Turning, with violent swipes of his massive paws, he took out his fury on the stand of saplings between them. The sound of wood snapping cut the air, sharp as gunfire. Trees broke at their bases, sent shards of wood flying, leaving ragged stumps, a section of forest that looked like it had been dynamited.

He had a clear path to her now. She stood exposed.

He rose on his hind legs. His nose, at the height of a two story window, sniffed the air trying to determine if she was predator or prey. He fell back on all fours and let out a roar that reverberated in her every corpuscle. She stayed crouched, hardly breathing.

Never look a bear in the eyes.

But her eyes would not obey.

He charged tearing through what remained in his way. She closed her eyes and thought *I'm dead.* She felt his massive presence, his hot breath on her, pumping fast, each moist breath parting the hair at the crown of her head.

Then nothing. Morey opened one eye, then the other.

The bear had retreated some twenty feet from her and sat there, watching. She ran her gaze over the ring of pale fur circling the giant chest, his muscle-humped shoulders and stopped at his massive head.

She looked into his small brown eyes and what she saw in them astonished her.

Acknowledgement.

He sniffed toward her, rose, turned and walked back through the devastation, his fur shimmering from side to side like wheat in sunlight and wind. He stopped at the edge of dense trees, turned his proud head back to her, waited.

Waited for her.

Morey pushed her muscles stiff with instinctive fear, stood and walked toward him. He turned and walked into the trees. The bear led her up the mountain, deeper and deeper into a wilderness she felt no human had traversed. Her legs ached from his pace. Up ahead, the dark backdrop of the extended forest gave way to a framed area of blue-white light as if the rest of the forest had simply disappeared. Moving toward the light Morey sensed a distinct change in the feel of the air, a lightness carried toward her on a soft wind.

The bear let her sit down not six feet from him and there, settled on their haunches, they looked out over a rim to the valley floor below, a valley with a river running through it, and bears. Many bears.

Morey stood by the cabin, backpack and carton at her feet, her camera clutched in her right hand. She would tell no one about the Valley of the Bears. About the bear that should have ripped her apart but instead saw something in her. She'd not betray his trust.

In her mind, the words of the dream repeated.

She has the magic.

The words chilled her. She felt like she didn't know anything anymore, not even herself. Her world had been altered and her need to know what the dream meant was all that mattered. She was certain her father held the key.

She heard the plane's droning engine before she saw it. A wing dipped and this time Claude circled before he brought the plane in for a landing. She stared down at her Canon containing evidence of the Sacred Valley of the Bears.

Claude waved at her to come, pointed up at the sky apparently worried about the light. She looked again at her camera then deleted all her work.

No one must know.

9

The Apoquaque ferry's metal floor vibrated under Morey's feet as it churned cold North Atlantic water. Despite the clear blue sky, the seas were high, and the small ferry rolled with the waves. She bungee-corded her bike to the starboard railing, then walked to the tip of the bow, passing the only other passengers, a man with his cup of coffee and daily newspaper, a woman with a well-worn paperback. Neither looked up. The tang of salt hit the back of her throat, sharp and acrid, the perfect accompaniment to the hollow ache that had taken up residence below her sternum.

She received the news on Tuesday at 4:15 p.m. She knew this exactly. She'd been waiting to board a 4:30 flight out of British Columbia to Chicago, a connector to Bangor, Maine, when her cell phone rang. She'd looked at her watch to see if she'd time to take the call. She was edgy, felt an anxiousness she attributed to her dread of visiting her father, especially unannounced. Their relationship was not hallmarked by casual drop-ins. The noise made her jump.

"Morey, I have bad news." It was Rupert Cirrus, dean of crusty old Braddard. She heard the clear, hollow tone of finality in his voice. She was hit by a sharp void that gives *time stopped* its meaning, and she knew immediately. Rupert apologized. He had tried, but she had been unreachable. Cremation, no wake, no funeral, her father's wishes.

A sudden heart attack - it was still so hard to believe. For days, she existed in a surreal state that she guessed was what others defined as shock. Francis Chance was gone, leaving her a strange sort of grief and unanswered questions about the dream that held her captive. Morey and her father had never nourished a father-daughter relationship.

Truth be told, they were more like acquaintances. On that rare visit to Braddard College, she stayed in a motel, never once entered his office, never attended a single one of his lectures. Their conversations were intellectual, her stays brief. Long ago, they'd closed an emotional door. She felt like a distant relative had died, taking with him the family secrets.

Morey grew up with a father who should never have been a parent. It didn't matter that they sat in the same room, on the same couch - the emotional distance was infinite. She hated the times she caught him watching her, studying her. He'd look away quickly, but there was no masking his anguish. She felt if her father's darkest wish had come true, she'd have disappeared. He did the next best thing; he went into hiding. As passionate as he was for archeology, she felt he used it to run from her. Rupert Cirrus had set her father up with a perfect schedule, a few classes, and an inordinate amount of time for field work. The Shelbyville Young Women's School became Morey's home.

Morey had been born on Apoquaque Island. Her father had told Morey her mother insisted on using a local midwife, despite his objections. She died giving birth to her. As a young child, she thought her father's coolness was her fault, that he blamed her for her mother's death, or that there was something wrong with her, maybe something she had acquired from her mother. She had a morbid fantasy that her mother was not dead but secretly locked up in an asylum. She saw herself, nose pressed up against a dirty window with thin black wire inside the glass, looking at a blurred, white-robed figure. The woman sat alone, head hung in inexpressible melancholy, hidden by cascades of long, dark hair. Then, as if she realized someone was there, the woman's head turned toward the window and through the curtain of hair, dark orbs stared back at Morey. As haunting as this image was, a crazy alive mother was better than a dead one.

There were summers though, summers on Apoquaque before her eleventh birthday, before Shelbyville. Times when she felt her father had tried. She remembered standing by her father on this very deck, both of them watching Apoquaque come into view. He'd held her small child's hand and through his grip, she'd sensed his love. But when they stepped ashore, something in him shifted, perhaps something only a child could sense, a vigilance grew in him, as if he had gone on guard, ready to keep something at bay.

The memory did not release her until she called Katherine Chance, her father's cousin; now Morey's only living relative. Those months she'd spent on Apoquaque at Aunt Katherine's, as she called her, while her father traveled back and forth to various digs, were her salvation. Her aunt said she had been waiting for Morey's call, that she'd get her old bedroom ready.

The sea had quieted. Above the metallic whine of the engine the sound of water sliced by the bow. She leaned into the railing, looked down at the swirling eddies appearing and disappearing where the hull cut the water, watched the water bend and float and close around the ferry. The sun's warmth on her shoulders made her sleepy, brought a sense of unreality she found comforting, as if she were asleep, peacefully asleep. She longed for a restful night's sleep free from the dream. She closed her eyes, thought of her father, let regret wash and recede.

She remembered fragments of her last day on Apoquaque. She was almost eleven years old, her birthday in one week, and she was alone with Aunt Katherine in the library. Her aunt was holding something in her hand, something cylindrical, shiny. Neither of them noticed her father enter. Morey remembered her aunt's expression changing when she looked up to see her father standing in the doorway. It was as if her face slowly melted. He told Morey to go to her bedroom in that voice of his that said he meant business. Then he closed the library door. Loud, angry voices followed. Morey and her father left that night and never returned. She pleaded each year to spend the summer on Apoquaque, but each summer her father scheduled a dig, and Morey remained at Shelbyville.

The engine lurched beneath her feet. Then the ferry went silent. She opened her eyes to see the fog bank. A huge gray mass waiting still on top of the water had swallowed up the world. The ferry slipped through the porous curtain into a dim, damp world. She turned. The two passengers, the captain's cabin, the entire back half of the ferry was gone from view.

"Gray ghost."

She heard the gruff voice first, and then a fireplug of a man stepped out of the fog, and stopped a few feet from her.

"That's the name given this fog," he said,

"A perfect name," she looked into a face etched by sea and sun, his small eyes black as the night. He was maybe in his forties; the elements aged those who made their living on the water. He wore a fisherman's rubber jacket, slick with condensation. It radiated cold. Then she noticed his boots, soaked, water dripped from them into a puddle at his feet.

"Caps smart to cut the engine, let the ship glide through. Many a sailor's at home beneath the gray ghost."

The thought gave Morey a chill. "She came out of nowhere."

"Cold current surrounds Apoquaque. When the warm air stills above it, the gray ghost does her mischief. I always like to come out and take a walk in her. Kind of friends we are. Beauty and danger make no mistake." The man then started to hum.

The sound came from his throat as if from hollow pipes. Despite the sweetness of the melody, Morey felt melancholy.

"Haunting. Do I know it?" she asked.

"Can't possibly. It's my song."

"You wrote it?"

"No," the pipes exhaled slowly. "No musical talent in the marrow of my bones. Our tradition," he glanced at her, and his look made her feel included, "Apoquaque people's ways. Never heard of the songs?"

"No, I'm afraid not."

"Well, when a mother's in her third month of pregnancy, she takes leave, goes and stays alone at a special place of her choosing. She asks the cosmos to reveal her baby's song to her. She must stay and wait patiently until she hears the song. Then each day, as the baby grows in her stomach, she sings his song to him. She sings his song to the father, the aunts and uncles, the community. Then at the child's birth, the town gathers to sing his song so the child will always know who he is."

The story struck a chord in her, a longing that for some reason made her sad. She wished she had a song.

"Morey Chance," she extended her hand, but he didn't take it.

"Can't never wash the fish smell off the hands of a fisherman. Sebastian Mott," he nodded once. "Going home?" he asked then turned, stared out into the fog.

"My aunt lives on the island." She followed his gaze. "I used to spend my summers here. But, yes, it feels like I'm going home."

"Aye, then you are. Not many are lucky enough to call Apoquaque home. She chooses us." He straightened up, and then his face changed. He looked forlorn. "Listen," he whispered.

For a moment she heard only the sound of the water lapping the hull. Then she heard the cries of sea gulls and the sound of what could only be breakers.

"Never enough time. Here she comes." He turned and walked toward the captain's station, disappearing into the mist. "Welcome home, Morey," she heard him call.

The fog broke, and Apoquaque loomed in front of her. Barren cliffs, rock-ribbed shoreline, the island rose from the water like a huge prehistoric sea monster. Black-backed gulls turned from their sentinel circles and headed like a guardian army toward the ferry.

Yes, she thought. *I am going home.* Suddenly she was overcome with the bizarre urge to throw her head back and give a full-throated howl like a wolf's song of homecoming. And she felt something else. She felt as if something inside of her, something long ago forgotten, was coming alive again.

10

The time since Hill left Africa seemed a blur. She had hated to leave, especially since they had gotten to Mbokwe, but she'd had no choice. There never was a choice. She always had to move on. Too many lives were at risk. Too much still had to be done. She stood in the cool surf, let it curl around her ankles, and listened to its receding hiss. Apoquaque Island seemed sullen today, or was it her own dark mood she sensed.

Charlie Dancer, a great hulk of a man, had helped load her crated equipment into the beached Zodiac. Hill looked at the crates stacked neatly in the Zodiac and laughed - all the pleasures of home. For whatever it was or wasn't, she had everything she needed. Later she would meet up with the others; some who lived on Apoquaque, some sent back home, as she had been, all knowing exactly what had to be done.

Charlie walked to Hill's side and looked out to sea. "That's about it. Last crate's in."

"Great. I'll start out then." There was a reedy, tired quality in her voice, a fatigue she could not hide. Hill stared at the Zodiac, feeling her inertia.

"All this'll wait till tomorrow." The great bear sensed her hesitation. "Tide's going out. The Zodiac will stay safely beached right here." Charlie looked up at the sky, pushed his massive shoulders back and straightened his spine, let out a groan. "Wife's got her famous fish stew on, and people have gathered in honor of your homecoming." He smiled his broad smile.

"Honor?" her tone was derisive. "They've gathered for the examination - a checkup to see if my failure has made me someone who can no longer be trusted with another mission."

Charlie looked embarrassed, stared at the horizon, shifting his weight as if he didn't know what to say.

"Another time," he muttered. "I'll tell them another time. No worries." He apparently knew when not to push things. He swung a heartfelt things-will-turn-out-fine poke into Hill's shoulder, then turned and walked into the surf. He waded through waist-high water till he reached his boat and easily climbed the rope ladder in. He started the up the thirty-foot Boston Whaler, then turned and waved.

Hill caught the questioning, concerned look on Charlie's face. She didn't like being the object of his solicitude. His sympathy was difficult for her to bear and could easily turn into pity. She would not tolerate pity from anyone. She bristled at the thought of being perceived as weak or unfortunate, and she had no capacity whatsoever for being patronized. Still, she didn't blame him. The community had called her home. She knew why. They needed to see if she could be trusted, if she could handle a mission without another costly mistake.

Hill watched Charlie pilot his Whaler out into open water. She admired Charlie's nautical skill, a skill shared by only a few men of the sea. In truth, Emma's fish stew had sounded delicious, and the last time she ate was early yesterday. She was famished, and she knew in her heart what she needed most was to reconnect with the community. But she felt she had been away too long, had seen too much, and at some point, somewhere, her desire to come home had died. It was not a conscious thing. It was more like some life force slowly evaporating, drying up, and disappearing without her knowledge. One day she awoke and realized it was gone. In its place was a terrible isolation. She felt like a sleepwalker who could no longer wake up.

It had been different once. Anchor was around. Her baby sister had been gifted. Her magic surpassed even hers. She could not stop the surge of anger she felt each time she thought of her. How could she have been so foolish? If she were with her today, she would shake her so hard, hold her so tight, make her promise to never…but she was gone.

Anchor had taken to the jump like no one else Hill had known. The first day she started lessons with her, Anchor was terrified of letting go, losing control. But once she accomplished her first jump, the miracle of it eclipsed her fears. From then on, Hill watched her grow into the most able of jumpers. Anchor could not get enough of it, wanted to try things that had never been done before, wanted to stay in the jump longer and longer.

Until the day she did not return.

Hill should have done something. She should have known better, seen the signs. Anchor was falling under its spell. Hill had warned her. But Anchor was so lighthearted, so carefree and trusting, full of life and love.

Anchor had always teased Hill, told her that she was too dreary, too cautious.

"Lighten up! You're taking all the fun out of this," she'd say as she ruffled Hill's hair.

"The jump is not supposed to be fun."

Hill had taught her little sister from childhood how important it was to pay attention. There were dangers. In the end, she felt it was she who had failed Anchor. She had been more than Anchor's big sister. She had been her teacher, responsible for her learning the tenets. She shouldn't have let her jump alone that day.

That day would haunt her the rest of her life. Anchor had wanted to jump all by herself, prove to her big sister she was capable, as good as she. Hill refused until she saw them in the area - government types, short military haircuts, dead, flat eyes, specialists of the worst kind. She knew they were looking for her, not Anchor. It was the closest they had ever gotten, much too close for her to jump. If the mission were to be successful, Anchor would have to do the jump alone.

Hill had made herself very visible that day, let them follow her, taken them far from the jump site, far enough that she could watch Anchor through her binoculars, far enough that Anchor would be safe from them.

But then something she hadn't counted on happened. Anchor's jump was almost over when through the binoculars Hill saw the dust funnel—Land Rovers kicking up sand and dirt as they sped to where Anchor was. They had sent others. They had known about Anchor too. She watched helplessly as they got closer and closer. If Anchor got back from the jump now, she would be all right. She would be able to get away before they arrived. But she was taking too much time, staying in the jump too long. Way too long. She knew what Anchor was doing. She was falling under its spell, letting the bewitching light and silence take her. Hill's mind screamed for Anchor to get back.

She watched as they took Anchor's body, placed it in one of the Land Rovers, and sped away.

She could do nothing.

She turned to the community, handed over to them her secret wish half-tainted with shame, pleaded with them to let her find those responsible, hunt them down. Their disapproval stung her. They reminded her of the tenet. *Do no harm.* Inside she felt nothing but rage. She had always been aware of injustice in the world but never before felt its twisting auger boring through her heart. The poignancy and purity of her anger consumed her. She tried to persuade them, arguing that the community must get Anchor's cylinder back, but she knew they saw through her. She knew they saw her true motivation, her pure, unadulterated need for revenge.

She knew too the community stood waiting ready to embrace her, that it was she who created her self-imposed exile, she who wanted to be left alone to lick her wounds. She stood no longer as a member of the community but in the twilight zone insistent on her status as a stranger. Yet deep down, where the truth inside oneself can be mined, she knew she was hiding from herself, scared they would see what she feared most - that she would never have the same heart she once had, that things were permanently realigned, her psyche rearranged, and a place for sadness interminably enlarged.

She heard the cry of a gannet, looked up and watched the bird, wings folded tight, plunge dive, slice the water like a knife. She knew there was more to the command that she return to the island. The community was gathering because Apoquaque needed protection. This made her return all the more bittersweet. And there was this nagging feeling that she could not shake off, that clung to her skin. She noticed it at the oddest moments, this feeling just out of her reach, something troubling she couldn't define - as if something unexpected was about to be added to the equation. It worried her. She heard a cry, far off, carried by the wind - a plaintive call much like a dog's howling. Then there was another long, light howl, and she was reminded that no matter what, she was a daughter of Apoquaque, that she could not let anything happen to her. She would die first.

11

Washington, DC

Stanley Protsky had seen this guy before. Feuer, John Feuer. That was his name.

"Where's the general's secretary, Elizabeth?" Protsky asked Feuer.

"Vacation." Feuer sat at Elizabeth's desk. He leaned far back into her chair, folded open the *Washington Post*, brought it up to block his view of Protsky, then flicked it hard.

Smart ass. Protsky looked at his watch. He'd been sitting for over two hours in the reception room of General Caleb's Pentagon office. His patience was wearing thin.

"How much longer?"

Feuer ignored him.

Protsky guessed Feuer had already figured out he lacked priority with the five-star general. Protsky did not belong to the elite club of military men with prestigious backgrounds and military postings. When the general was damn good and ready, he would call him in.

General James Hecht walked stiffly into the reception room. He moved past Protsky and immediately into the general's office, the business at hand much too important to waste time acknowledging Protsky's presence.

Protsky detested them, these tall, well-built, elite military men whom women watched, hungered for, dreamed about. Women looked somewhere else when they saw Protsky coming. He was short, overweight, a prime candidate for a heart attack, yet as unfortunate as his physical appearance might be, he had something the others could never attain, something they could only dream about - an off-the-Richter scale IQ. He smiled, pleased at the thought that in a millisecond, he could outsmart any of them.

Protsky glanced at the front page of Feuer's paper, read the headline: <u>Graham's Testimony at Predator Congressional Hearing Ends</u>. Then he remembered the first time he'd seen Feuer. Two months ago, at three in the morning, he had received a call to report immediately to the Hotel Sofitel, Suite 113. He'd knocked on the door and was let in by a man with a military buzz, a National Security Agency card with his name on it hanging from his jacket's breast pocket. John Feuer. Feuer frisked him, and then led him down a short corridor to the suite's interior.

"Mr. Graham, sir. Dr. Protsky has arrived." Feuer left Protsky standing there and headed back to the front door.

If Protsky had not caught the televised congressional hearings, he would have been shocked. Snow-white hair cropped close to the scalp and albino complexion gave Gabriel Graham the look of a man who had never seen daylight. In the hotel room Graham sat in front of a laptop, impenetrable sunglasses hid his eyes.

Protsky looked around the hotel suite. Large, elegantly decorated. A blank blackboard on rollers stood to the left of the table where Graham sat. To the left of the blackboard on a column, a lit glass box about a foot square contained something shiny. On a buffet table to the right were several unopened Perrier bottles, a table setting, and untouched covered dishes.

"Help yourself." Graham had not moved, but apparently, he had been watching Protsky through his darkened lenses.

"No, thank you."

"Yes, looks like you've already eaten."

The corner of Graham's mouth curled up so slightly Protsky could almost have missed it. Protsky had wanted to say *screw you* but was smart enough to keep quiet.

"You're here to give me a physics lesson." Graham raised a linen-white hand, pointed to the blackboard. His hands were beautiful, perfect hands for a pianist, long fingers, nails perfectly shaped, clean. "Chalk's there when you need it."

Graham questioned Protsky about Einstein's equations, the time-space continuum, negative mass, wormholes, quantum physics. Untiringly, he digested information quickly, manipulated concepts with genius. At the end of three hours, Graham said simply, "If I need more, I'll send for you."

Feuer led Protsky out. That was the last time he'd seen Feuer - until now.

Protsky walked over to Elizabeth's desk, craned his neck, tried to read the *Washington Post* column about Graham. Feuer flicked the paper hard, like an annoying fly had landed on it. Protsky grunted, shuffled back to his seat. He had watched the congressional hearings with great interest. Graham was intense, cool, flatly refused to take off his sunglasses citing coloboma, a congenital condition that made light painful. Graham sat alone at a long table, took the heat for a new software system that allowed the National Security Agency to read private e-mail. Graham, appropriately enough, had named the NSA system Predator. He defended the system as a necessary tool for ridding the Internet of terrorists, crooks, and child pornographers. He refused to release the underlying programming or source code, angering the senators of the committee.

"The potential for abuse here is tremendous," Senator John Staeller had said at the hearings. "What you're saying is - trust us."

Protsky had heard of other special assignments with Graham's signature, none with pretty endings. Graham's covert activities were hallmarked by brilliant planning, a take-no-prisoners mindset, and a reputation for unfettered viciousness. Even the president was protected from knowledge of Graham's projects.

General Whitehall, a gargantuan soldier whose size suggested to Protsky a gorilla in military garb, strode into the reception room, past Feuer. "Hear it's happening again," he tossed toward Protsky, and then walked into the general's office.

Protsky already knew it was happening again. Data had begun pouring out of his computer since 5:17 a.m. He knew too that behind the general's massive office doors, they were deciding just how much to tell him. When they did they would open the doors, let him in, and ask his opinion. His role was to explain the inexplicable. An ex-Harvard physics professor, he attempted to educate, struggled to simplify for them the forces of the universe. It was a supreme challenge to make clear what he considered was intellectually and scientifically out of their grasp. What did these men know about quantum physics?

Yet somewhere, someone, more likely some group knew a great deal about quantum physics. More than any other human being had yet grasped. Hell, even the finest scientists were light years behind what this group knew. What mystified him was what was this group was waiting for? Knowledge like this meant unequivocal world domination, power with an atomic-blast-your-socks-off capital P.

The phone buzzed. Feuer picked it up, glanced at Protsky. "Your turn," his tone was snide.

Protsky entered the general's office and immediately felt his body go rigid. Whitehall and Hecht sat at the general's table as expected, but at the head of the table, in General Caleb's seat, was Gabriel Graham.

"Dr. Protsky," Graham smiled, "come in." He turned to the others. "Sorry, gentlemen, this is where you get off."

General Hecht flushed. "How dare you, sir."

"You're playing with fire, Graham." General Whitehall rose from his chair almost tipping it over.

"My favorite game," Graham said flatly.

General Hecht stood, tugged down his uniform jacket, and followed General Whitehall out of the office. The door slammed after them.

"Generals, no real guts." Graham pushed his shoulders back and took in a deep breath of air as if it were the freshest air he had ever breathed. "Good to see you again, Protsky." Graham opened the laptop on the desk in front of him, punched a few keys. The wall behind Graham slid open on rollers, exposing a small room devoid of furniture. In it was that column with the lit glass box.

"I've got a job for you, something suited to a man of your intelligence." Graham's elbows were on the table, his long alabaster fingers touching each other, tip to tip, like a spider on a mirror. Protsky sensed Graham enjoyed the camaraderie of equal intellect, a kinship among geniuses, and was intolerant of stupidity.

"The project you've been working on—did you know it was I who assigned you?" Graham said.

Protsky was about to say no, but Graham continued.

"Every report you've written for General Caleb was for me. Impressive detail," Graham yawned. "Excuse me. Generals bore the shit out of me. No imagination. But the phenomena you've been studying, miraculous," his voice lifted. He pulled a flash drive out of the laptop, tossed it over the table to Protsky.

Protsky juggled the flash drive in his hands, almost dropped it.

"The information on the flash drive will catch you up. I've kept you in the dark on some matters." Graham rose from his chair, walked toward the glass box. For the first time, Protsky saw Graham not seated. He was tall, slender. His walk was awkward, like he had broken some bones that had never set properly. His body tilted slightly forward, his arms hanging in front of his body as if he were about to spring onto something. Protsky couldn't help but glance at the floor.

"Ever see anything like it?" Graham gestured to what was inside the glass box.

Protsky slipped the flash drive into his breast pocket, walked to the column, and looked inside the glass box at a cylinder. He noticed symbols etched into it, characters like hieroglyphics.

"Some kind of Egyptian artifact?" Protsky asked.

"The artifact and the phenomena are connected," Graham ignored his question. "I want you to figure out how."

Graham circled back to the table, opened up a photograph on the laptop screen, motioned Protsky over.

Protsky walked over to the table and looked at it. The photograph was of a young woman, obviously deceased. Protsky felt a bead of sweat form on his forehead. He looked at Graham. Graham's facial expressions rarely changed. Protsky wondered if this was deliberate or if the man was simply dead inside.

"First name's Anchor, last name unknown. The cylinder was hers. Too bad, such a pretty young thing," Graham said without emotion. Then he was silent.

Protsky sensed the intermission was intentional, meant to add emphasis to what Graham was going to say next.

"A casualty of acquiring the cylinder, nothing of course for you to worry about," Graham finished.

A burning pain moved from Protsky's stomach to his throat and he tasted the sour digested remains of his lunch.

12

Apoquaque Island

Morey slipped on her backpack, released the bungee cord from her bike, and surveyed Apoquaque's small harbor. Fathers, sons, and daughters still fished these waters, up so early each day that their boats were noticeably vacant from the harbor. Only a few small craft dotted the port and swayed gently in the ferry's wake. Morey looked down into the green ocean water, its surface alive with the play of sunlight, its unpolluted depths rich with life. She had seen her first sea lions frolicking here off Little Apoquaque, a mere speck of rock and pebbles in the ocean northeast of Apoquaque Main.

She watched the two other ferry passengers disembark in silence and walk down the pier toward town. Apoquaque islanders, she remembered them all too well. Centuries of isolation had produced generations of rugged survivors fiercely protective of their privacy and their island. The two passed an old hut with a sign reading BAIT hanging askew on rusted chains, its door closed, then came to a sudden stop. Two large wolf-like dogs loped into view. Morey watched the man and woman hesitate, then walk wide around the dogs and disappear around the back of the hut. The larger dog of the pair, perhaps the male, snorted dismissively. Then the two sat down, alert, shoulder to shoulder.

She negotiated her bike down the ramp and onto the pier, not taking her eyes off the dogs. They were definitely wild. She saw the hunter in their sharp amber eyes. The larger dog's eyes flickered toward a rustling noise. Caught in the beach grass, a piece of torn newspaper moved in the off-shore breeze. In black block print, apparently a head-line, the letters read STOP SATURN OIL. She looked back at the dogs, both intently focused on her now, and for a moment, an uncanny thought crossed her mind. The dogs knew what the headline meant and wanted her to read it.

She scanned the area. The pier ended at the hut, and from there was one road, only one way to go, no other choice. She mounted her bike, pedaled closer. The dogs watched her approach; rose off their haunches, muscles like springs ready to explode. She heard a thin cry of doggy excitement from the female. Not taking any chances, when she was within fifteen feet she pumped as hard as she could and sped past them, giving them a wide birth. When she felt safe enough, she turned back and watched the two stretch their sinewy bodies and trot after her. She decided whatever the dogs wanted they meant her no harm. The two easily caught up to her and ran alongside her bike, adjusting their speed to hers. She watched their fluid motion, these animals of sinew and strength. She glided for a moment, listened to their panting. Their company was welcome.

She rode the abrupt hills and deep descents through acres of open land spotted by small stands of trees and brambles of serpentine brush. A farmhouse set far back from the road appeared every half mile or so. Here and there small groups of horses or goats nibbled on alfalfa. She used to sit in these fields of tall grasses surrounded by the lazy buzz of insects and the sound of the horses' slow chewing. Sometimes, when the air was still, the wood ducks' choral from the marshes reached her ears. God, she'd missed this island. It was one of those rare and beauti-ful places known only to the local people and never taken for granted by them. When her father had abruptly left with her in tow that sum-mer night long ago, she'd felt in exile. Now she wondered why she had waited so long to return.

The dogs panted rhythmically, tongues flapping happily from the sides of their mouths. Morey rounded a curve, and the Victorian came into view. How little the house had changed. Two hickory-and-cane rockers sat on the porch, just as she remembered. The windows of the house were open wide. A breeze blew through the house and out a porch window, carrying with it a wisp of white lace curtain, twisting it up and fluttering it, setting one of the rockers into gentle motion. She felt a wave of nostalgia. Then something quite different tugged at her mind, like a memory that had receded too deeply to mine. She remembered her father's tight grip on her small child's hand as they stepped off that long-ago ferry and came ashore. She felt her stomach tighten. She didn't like the feeling.

Morey pumped up the gravel driveway. She swung her long leg over the bicycle seat, knocked down the kickstand. She took a quick look in the bike's mirror. Her face flushed from the ride, made the dark circles under her eyes, the badge of sleepless nights, more noticeable. She ran her fingers through tangled short hair and decided it was as good as she could get it. She looked around just in time to see two dog tails disappear into the meadow of tall wild prairie grass across the road from the house.

"Deserters!" she called. She dropped her backpack, squeezed the bike's horn.

She heard the sound of a shovel entering earth. "Wait there!"

Morey looked to the left of the house where the ground rose then leveled off in a garden plot. There in the middle of rich, dark, overturned earth, in a pair of oversized gardening overalls and green rubber boots, stood Aunt Katherine, hand atop her shovel. Her hair had turned a translucent white, and she looked smaller than Morey remembered.

Katherine tossed down her gardening gloves and walked briskly to meet Morey. There was vitality to her movement that made her seem younger than her age, living proof that staying true to yourself helped you stay young.

"Look at you," Katherine took Morey's hands. Her eyes, set in nests of fine wrinkles, gleamed with energy and mischief. "You're beautiful." The smell of warm, ripe earth like baked bread surrounded them. Katherine took a step back, looked her over head to toe. "No, you're stunning."

Morey felt her face flush. "You're biased."

"Who better to be biased about?" Katherine placed an arm around her.

Morey liked the feel of the old woman's arm. It gave her a comforting sense of continuity with her past. Aunt Katherine was enduring. Somebody you could count on.

Katherine guided Morey up the porch steps, stopped by a rocker, sat down, and kicked off her boots. "It's been way too long." There was a question in her tone that made Morey feel ashamed she had waited so long to return.

"Life's timing is not always up to us," Katherine said, as if she had read Morey's mind.

"I've never forgotten this place, or you." Her words felt hollow. Morey knew this was no excuse.

She walked the old porch. The same floorboards squeaked and groaned. She glided her hand along the porch railing, smooth, sturdy. She wondered what would have happened if she had stayed here.

"I'm going to wash up." Katherine brushed a smear of black soil from her overalls. "Start cooking us a hot supper." She rose, studied Morey's face. "You look exhausted."

"I haven't been sleeping well lately."

"Perhaps we can do something about that. You're home now. Get your things up to your old bedroom, Bucket." She waved Morey off, disappeared into the Victorian.

"Bucket," Morey repeated softly. She smiled. As a child, she had sat for hours on end on an old milking stool by the barn at the back of the house. Her gangly legs straddled the huge rain barrel that collected runoff from the barn's steep roof. Hunched over it, elbows resting on its rim, face pushed by small fists, its still, dark reflective waters produced the only screen needed for her active imagination. Plunk in a pebble, the world changed. Her young mouth had trouble with Rs and Ls, so *barrel* became *bucket*.

Her aunt had said she could see Morey's inner world in the dark, reflective pools of Morey's eyes. Morey's eyes, Katherine had said, were Katherine's bucket.

Another world. Another time. Or was it?

Morey retrieved her bags and walked into the Victorian. Wood cut and shipped from the Americas, mostly mahogany and cherry, warmed the interior. She stopped in the middle of the central hall, the hub of the house. The dining room and kitchen were to the left, sitting room and library to the right, the wide stairway to the second floor straight ahead. She climbed the stairs, stood on the landing, and looked down the second floor hallway of bedrooms and baths. Katherine's bedroom was the first door on the right, her father's old room, last door on the left. Immediately opposite his room a narrow staircase spiraled to the tower room.

Squeezing herself and her bags up the spiral staircase, Morey recalled how much larger the space had seemed when she was a child. She stopped at the top, hesitated on the landing before the open door. She looked in. A bed, a standalone full-length mirror, and an armoire were the only furniture in the room. Late-afternoon light washed through the window, bathed the room in a golden glow. She was reminded again of something lost, not remembered. Then a peculiar sensation rushed through her. A prickly anxiety rose in her chest. She trusted her instincts, what they were telling her. Something had waited all these years for her return.

She stepped into the room and dropped her bags on the bed. Small as the tower room was its three-pane bay window took up one quarter of the circular room's walls, creating the illusion of a larger space. She walked to the window and looked down at the dark earth of Katherine's garden, beyond to the greenhouse where Katherine had started her summer crop, the tangle of raspberry bushes now only twisted canes. Barn. Tool shed. Surrounding forest. She was eleven again, shoeless, damp grass tickling chill between her toes, running on thin pole legs toward the margin of the pine forest to a memory her little girl body felt so drawn.

There had been children her age on the island, but Morey had rarely played with them. She had preferred to spend her days alone in the forest or fields, on the beach. Never lonely, she'd been quite content. Apoquaque was the only friend she'd needed. She'd been a strange child, caught up in her imagination, insistent upon her secrets. Yet she knew all too well there was more to her chosen solitude. Her fantasies had been vivid, too vivid. There were times when she had been unable to distinguish between imagination and reality. Even at her young age, she'd known she couldn't speak about it. She'd been pretty certain other children didn't conjure up such things in their minds. Yet Morey felt Katherine somehow knew about it all. At first this troubled her, but eventually it forged a strong communion Morey shared with no one else.

She remembered the day Katherine startled her, caught her daydreaming. She'd put her hands on Morey's shoulders, moved her face close, spoke with intensity. "Morey, don't ever run from what's in your mind. Go into it. Get to know it. Then you're really who you are. Only then. Will you remember this?"

What she remembered was that Katherine gave her the comfort of acceptance and understanding. It was Morey's salvation.

The smell of roast chicken rose up the stairwell. God, she was hungry. She walked down the stairs and followed the aroma to the kitchen, stopped just inside.

"Hope you don't mind having dinner in the kitchen." Katherine opened the oven door, peered in.

"Sounds great," Morey looked around. The round oak table, nestled into a floor-to-ceiling bow window, was set for dinner. A wooden bowl was filled with fresh salad greens. There wasn't much for her to do.

"Dining room's too formal, better left for company." With mittened hands, Katherine pulled a steaming chicken from the oven and placed it on the stove.

Katherine's kitchen reflected her personality perfectly. In the center stood a massive butcher block Katherine had built from an oak windfall. At its center, there was a smooth depression worn by years of chopping and cutting. Dried herbs and copper pots hung from ceiling racks. The smell of garlic mixed with a hint of turpentine that Morey guessed was from one of Katherine's recent projects hung in the air. The cabinets, painted a dark green, had the uneven look of several layers of paint on top of one another. Morey remembered Katherine was always changing things. Next to the iron gas stove was the deep, angled soapstone sink Morey had bathed in as a small child. Above, on a shelf was a jar filled with dried beans. Leaning against it was the slingshot Katherine used to keep feral cats from fledgling birds. Stuck in the wall with a thumb tack was the black and white photograph of a pine tree Morey had taken with her first camera, a Polaroid she'd found in a drawer. The kitchen was full of lived-in memories.

Across the room from the table, a small desk was covered with papers Morey guessed to be correspondence, bills. There was no cell tower on the island so she was surprised to see a laptop and a scanner. She followed the laptop's wires to the telephone jack. "Aunt Katherine, you do e-mail?"

"Don't get fresh with me. I'm not some throw-back to the Ice Age." She poked the chicken with a fork. Its juices ran warm onto the platter.

The shelf above the desk was loaded with books on gardening and cooking. Morey spotted the old Polaroid sitting on *Herbs That Heal* and picked it up.

"Wow, look at this antique," she pulled film from an opened box and loaded the camera.

"That's vintage, not antique." Katherine feigned annoyance.

Morey edged close to her aunt, leaned her face next to hers, stretched the camera out in front of them, and clicked, the flash surprising even her.

Katherine gave Morey a sharp jab in the ribs with a bony elbow. "Do something constructive. Open a bottle of wine. Dinner's about ready."

Looking at the Polaroid shot propped up against the half-empty bottle of Glen Ridge Cabernet, Morey found herself grinning about how much it looked like one of those awful snapshots from inside a picture-for-a-buck booth. The black and white photo accentuated her dark circles, which in turn set off her eyes, eyes she thought a smidge too large, a bit too dark. She studied her image, her face. Somewhere in there was her mother.

Her father had always told Morey she was beautiful, just like her mother, a mother Morey never knew. At a very young age, Morey had given up asking her father questions about her. Could she see a picture of her? What was she like? Her questions were answered only by eyes glazed with distress, then silence as if he were retreating to some secret place no one else was allowed to go.

As much as she'd longed for some tangible evidence of her mother, the very center of her being cowered from it. She'd sensed immediately that in life there are secret doors you did not open, dark nights you did not step out in unless you could withstand the whirlwind. Whenever she pushed her father, every corpuscle within her became terrified of what she might find out. There was something terribly wrong about her mother, some hideous secret. Finding out would mean she'd become tainted by it, become sick with it, become hideous too. It was, she'd come to admit, she too who kept her mother's ghost trapped in the narrow emptiness between this world and the next. Morey had figured out long ago that a great deal of her adult bravado, her risk-taking behavior, was her trying to forget her inner river of cowardice.

"A penny for your thoughts," Katherine said.

"Dad," Morey felt the familiar unease in her chest, the small child hesitating at the doorway of a room she should not enter, "why would he never speak of my mother?"

Katherine moved in her seat. "You should have asked your father that question."

"It wouldn't have helped." She sounded like a quitter. She didn't like it. "Do you know if my mother," she hesitated, "heard voices?"

Katherine's eyebrows shot up. She stared at Morey.

"You know." Morey raised a hand to her temple, made a circular movement with her index finger.

Katherine looked miffed. "I, for one, hear voices all the time. Whispers in the wind. Why the other day—"

"I'm not joking."

"Neither am I." Katherine's voice was forceful. "Hearing voices, perhaps it's…" she paused, apparently searching for the right word, "a gift."

"Gift? More like insanity."

"Glass half-empty, glass half-full. History is replete with brilliant people whom their times labeled crazy."

Morey looked down at her plate, then back up at Katherine. "Something is happening to me." She brought her voice low. "You know I've always been different."

Katherine's face looked pained, but she said nothing.

"This, this dream has come back. It won't let me rest. A voice in the dream, I think it's my mother's."

"Your mother's? What does the voice say?"

"She has the magic."

Morey saw it in her aunt's eyes, distant and unfocused, her entering a hallway of memory. Then Katherine pushed her chair away from the table and stood, startling Morey. "I have something for you," she said, then left the kitchen.

Morey heard her aunt's footfalls in the central hall, the library's mahogany sliding doors opening. Surprised, she felt her heart racing.

Her aunt reappeared in the doorway, holding something in her hand. On the table next to Morey's wine glass, Katherine placed an oblong black velvet bag tied at the top with a drawstring. "This was left for you," she said stone-faced, then sat down.

Morey stared at the velvet bag. "Who left it for me?"

"Your mother."

Morey felt a shudder go through her body. What was that expression about someone walking on your grave?

"Your father," Katherine hesitated, then began again. "Your father kept it all these years. He mailed it to me just weeks before his death, wanted you to have it for your birthday, wrote that you were somewhere unreachable, on a photo shoot."

Morey stared at the bag, heart pounding. She picked up the bag, felt something hard inside. She loosened the string, tilted the bag. Into her left hand she slid a cylinder about five inches long, two in diameter. It was smooth, shiny. It appeared to be bone, maybe ivory. But unlike the expected coolness of bone, it was warm, almost like something alive. She rotated the cylinder and found an inscription etched into it. The writing looked like some kind of hieroglyphics. Morey studied the symbols from every angle. Nothing helped. It was clearly a language different from any she'd ever seen. She rotated the cylinder again, examined it closely, and noticed a thin, continuous line length-wise around the cylinder, as if it were meant to open. She looked for a way to open it, gently tried to pry it open with her hands. It would not budge.

She laid it back on the table and noticed the tip of a piece of paper jutting out from the velvet bag. She grabbed the edge, pulled it loose, and stared down at her father's handwriting.

"The greatest theft of all is to rob one of the right to be," she read aloud. "What does that mean?" She looked up at Katherine. "Did my father say anything, write anything else?"

"Nothing."

"Not why he kept it all these years?"

"Not a word."

"Not what this inscription means?"

"No."

Morey returned her gaze to the cylinder. "It looks as if it's meant to open. But what's top, what's bottom?"

"Looks like your mother left you a mystery," Katherine said, then picked up her fork, stabbed a piece of lettuce, pushed it into her mouth.

"That's it!" Morey said louder than she'd intended.

Katherine munched on the lettuce, looked at her.

"I never knew my mother. No one ever talked about her. Then suddenly this gift, this thing—"

"Seems strange, I know."

"Strange isn't the word for it. What was she? A serial killer? A schizophrenic locked away in an asylum? That's what Dad was so afraid of - latent family lunacy." Morey spoke her deepest fear.

"Don't be silly." Katherine reached for Morey's hand and held it. "This cylinder is your birthright." She let go of Morey's hand. Morey watched her move her hand across the table, then to her lap. Katherine had the look of someone who had said too much.

Morey was shocked. Her aunt knew more than she was telling. "Birthright, what are you saying?"

Katherine straightened in her chair. "Morey, you must be patient about some things."

"Patient." If she weren't so exasperated, she'd laugh. "I'm twenty-five years old. That makes twenty-five years of patience."

"You see? That's not such a long time."

"Aunt Katherine!"

"There'll be no more talk about this tonight, young lady." Katherine stood, took her plate to the sink. "Certain things you must find out for yourself. You've always been good at that. Besides, they have more meaning that way. Now help me clean up." Katherine turned on the faucet, her back to Morey, her posture rigid.

Morey knew this discussion was over. *Stubborn old lady*, she fumed to herself.

Morey sat curled up on the bench nestled into the tower room window, arms hugging her legs to her chest, her head resting on her knees, the cylinder in her hand. After all these years, years of not hearing even a word about her mother, and now she held a gift from her in her hand - this peculiar gift with no explanation.

Morey looked out the window. The night was perfect, filled with stars. She leaned her head against the glass. Her breath condensed on it, forming a silvery film. She placed a finger on it, melting a small hole. She shivered, not from the cold but from the sense her world was transforming. She had come back to Apoquaque seeking answers. Her father gone, she had nowhere else to turn.

The greatest theft of all is to rob one of the right to be.

What did this message from her father mean? She thought of her recurring dream. What if it had not been a dream at all? She had come to believe her father knew something, something that scared him, and he felt the need to protect her. She took one last look out the window;

a shooting star passed in the dark. Exhausted, she fell into a deep sleep and dreamed.

Morey stood inside the tool shed, the door opened, her mother next to her. Outside a storm raged.

"Your father was afraid, my dear."

"Afraid? Afraid of what?"

"Afraid you will become me."

13

Braddard College

Dean Rupert Cirrus sat in an overstuffed chair in his study, feeling the effects of his second Scotch. On the table next to him sat his glass and a Waterford decanter of Macallan. Alcohol helped soothed the sadness. Scattered about the floor were cartons he had Vito, the custodian move from Francis's office before the college closed it up. He had spent years watching Francis's career, Francis's anguish. At the retirement dinner, the last time he was with Francis, he'd toasted to his genius. He'd meant every word. He knew him in the early years when Francis's fieldwork had earned him a reputation for persistence and uncompromising exactness. He had a gift for solving the most exasperatingly complex archeological puzzles. Rupert had no doubt that if Francis's life had been different, he would have been the most respected archeologist in the world instead of an obscure crazy man in the annals of archeology.

They'd met what felt like lifetimes ago, a million miles away on the Buttu Highlands. They were excavating a thousand-year-old African village. Francis was in charge of a small army of archeologists troweling, brushing the foundation of an ancient tribal dwelling, recovering animal bones, clay vessels, plant remains. Rupert was Francis's second-in-command.

The dig was on a plain at the base of a mountain covered by dense rainforest. Unusual weather struck. A tremendous rainstorm pelted the site. Everyone worked furiously to protect fragile artifacts. Exhausted, the crew retired early. Hours before dawn, an African guide stole into their tent, woke them, and begged them to follow him into the rainforest. Within the jungle, the guide said, the rainstorm had unearthed a most miraculous place, hallowed ground.

The two of them followed the guide through the camp, macheted their way through thick jungle undergrowth. Finally, at a rim overlooking a steep valley, the guide stopped. The sun was just coming up over the rim; its rays slowly vaporized the gray mist fingering through the forest. The guide pointed straight down into the valley to where the valley walls made an elbow turn. One look at the terrain, and it was obvious. The night's torrential rain had funneled into a raging slide of water that had raced down from the mountains and scoured the valley floor. At the turn where the valley walls bent, the water had crashed into its walls forming a vicious stripping whirlpool. They looked down upon a huge circular barren area of drying mud and silt the size of a small lake and saw the most incredible sight.

Rupert picked up his glass, took another sip of Scotch, felt its warmth slide down his throat. He glanced down at the opened journal resting on his lap. He had retrieved it from one of Francis's cardboard cartons, spent the night reading it. It was Francis's account of the Buttu Highland dig. Francis's script had drawn him back in time. He remembered the excitement of that morning. He read the script aloud.

It laid before us, mesmerizing and miraculous in the jungle silence, everything so still as if a sacred battlefield had been unearthed. The bones of hundreds of beasts, buried in the forgotten pockets of time, seams worn open, jutted out from the caking mud.

Rupert tried to fight off his sadness. Even then, that day, as Francis showed him the artifact, Rupert knew it would mean Francis's doom.

They made it back to the excavation site by dusk. Francis summoned the team of archeologists and excitedly revealed what they had found. That evening another rainstorm hit, and the next morning when Francis returned with his fellow archeologists, the mystical site had been washed clean. All evidence extinguished. But Francis had the cylinder.

The news burst upon the archeological world like a bombshell. Francis was the new wunderkind. He believed he had discovered an unknown ancient culture that had communed with the animals. The cylinder would be tested to determine its age. The glyphs were undecipherable, clearly from an undiscovered language. Linguist after linguist attacked the problem seemingly more intractable than the Rosetta stone.

Then the news hit like a fist. The cylinder was a fake. It carbon 14 tested as not more than several hundred years old. Francis was accused of the worst sin of the archeological world: a hoax. No one would touch him after that. He applied to hundreds of digs. Most letters came back unopened. Rupert's offer to teach at Braddard was Francis's last chance to stay close to his life's calling. Having Francis at Braddard kept Rupert close to the artifact. He knew if Francis did not decode the glyphs, no one would.

Rupert watched Francis's obsession with cracking the glyphs grow to border on madness. His specialty became epigraphy, the deciphering of ancient script. Francis mastered Ethiopic, Sanskrit, Zend, Pahlevi, Arabic, Syrian, Chaldean, and Persian. The mystery of the glyphs consumed him, left him little energy for anything or anyone else. Francis showed up at digs that held even the remotest chance of connection with the ancient language etched into the cylinder. Uninvited, soon asked to leave. Feeling pity for his friend, he began using Braddard's funds to finance Francis's own digs. Always returning to lock himself in his study, Francis barely ate, rarely taught, consume himself with nothing but research. Days, nights, years into deciphering the ancient symbols, trying to crack the miniature jigsaw puzzle over and over again frustrated, Francis hit wall after wall.

Then came Apoquaque and Morey.

Rupert understood the demons that tormented Francis. Francis was born for this work. Every neuron of his brain hungered for it, yet every fiber of his heart condemned him. Francis was caught in the unkindest of traps. To crack the glyphs, to prove the cylinder a true artifact, not a fake, to redeem himself, he risked exposing his daughter.

Rupert picked up the table lighter, flicked it. A hint of butane hit his nostrils. He stared for a moment into the yellow flame, then tilted the journal's edge into it. He watched the journal smolder, blacken around its edge, watched the paper curl into the growing flame. He rose and walked to the fireplace. He held the burning journal till the flames almost burned his fingers, the pain somehow satisfying, then dropped it onto the grate. He stood transfixed, watched the consuming flames until there was nothing but blackened ash.

14

Morey awoke trying to capture the wisps of a dream. Something about it left her feeling ill at ease. Then came the warm wash of realization that it had not been *that* dream. She turned over to go back to sleep, then shot up in bed as if lightening had stuck her. Her aunt's laptop, the Polaroid.

She looked outside, guessed it was five, maybe five-thirty. She slipped from bed and hurried to get dressed. Sneakers in hand, she tiptoed down the staircase to the second floor landing. She listened. Silence. Katherine was still asleep. Morey heard the ticking of the grandfather clock in the central hall, went down the stairs into the hall, its walls washed with the light of the breaking dawn.

She padded along into the kitchen, slipped on her sneakers, and laced them up.

She went to her aunt's desk and raised the lid of the laptop. The laptop came to life with a whiney whistle and the Microsoft Windows logo filled the screen. Icons up, she clicked the mouse on Internet Explorer, went to Google, and then in the search box she typed "cylindrical artifact with ancient inscribed script."

There were fifteen pages of websites. Amusingly, there was one on paperclips and of course, a veritable supermarket of supposed ancient artifacts for sale. One sounded promising. She opened a page entitled: Archeological Digs, Buttu Highlands, Uganda.

It was just what she was looking for. This website was built by and for archeologists. She began to read.

Scholarly interest in the highland area increased during the late twentieth century promoting three exploratory expeditions to the region: Morwood (1959–60), Parrot (1970–1971), and Chance (1987–1989). Intensive archeological research began when Chance extended his excavation twenty-five kilometers northwest of Morwood's.

Chance (1987-1989). Could this be her father? If so, this was before she was born.

Morey scrolled down, scanning the summaries of Morwood's, then Parrot's excavations including detailed maps, analysis of fauna bone fragments, flora, and stone material, sediment analysis, and radiocarbon dating. The technical words were familiar, many she'd heard from her father, but much of the information was beyond her reach. It was the summary concerning the Chance excavation and its contact information she found astonishing.

Chance did not publish his excavation. General comment has attributed this lack of publication to problems during the excavation believed to have resulted in misidentification of excavated material (see Buttu Cylinder). Still, papers describing two preliminary analyses on stone and bone material are available from Braddard College, Department of Archeology, Braddard, Maine. For information concerning the cylindrical artifact, please contact Rupert Cirrus at CirrusR@Braddard.edu.

This *was* her father's dig. The cylinder was found at this dig. And Rupert Cirrus knew something about it. Morey thought for a moment. She pulled the cylinder from her overall pocket, placed it on the kitchen table where the light was strongest, picked up the Polaroid, and snapped a picture. She placed the Polaroid picture in the scanner, scanned it, and sent the picture to e-mail. She started to type.

Dear Dean Cirrus,

My father always spoke highly of your friendship so I hope what I am about to ask is not an imposition. I have recently acquired a cylindrical artifact etched with hieroglyphics sent to me by my father. I am most interested in information about its origin, if possible a translation of its hieroglyphics. Perhaps you can help or know of someone within the university's department of archeology who can assist me. Please scroll to a picture of the artifact. Please send response to this e-mail address, as I am currently with my aunt on Apoquaque Island.

Thank you for any assistance you can offer.

Morey Chance

She read it over. Satisfied, she clicked send.

She went back to Google, typed in "Buttu Cylinder," and found it in Wikipedia.

The Buttu Cylinder was a hoax in which a cylinder was presented as an artifact of an unknown early human culture. The artifact was collected by archeologist Frances Chance in a remote jungle area of the Buttu Highlands, Uganda. It was exposed by carbon dating as a fake.

Previous to its exposure as a fake, the cylinder captured the imagination of amateur and professional archeologists, and many attempts to decipher its symbols failed. While it was not clear that the symbols were a script, most attempted decipherments assumed that it was and it was generally thought that decipherment was unlikely to be successful unless more examples of the symbols were found, as it was generally agreed that there was not enough context available for meaningful analysis.

Although the Buttu Cylinder is accepted as a fake, a few scholars have forwarded the opinion that the artifact, although not as old as first reported, is authentic and significant. The argument remains moot, as the cylinder was lost.

She reviewed what she had learned. Her father had unearthed the cylinder during his dig on the Buttu Highlands before her birth. He believed the cylinder to be an artifact of an unknown early human culture. Many tried but failed to decipher its hieroglyphics. It was deemed a fake. It was lost. Until now? Her father had sent it to her, care of Aunt Katherine with a note: *The greatest theft of all is to rob one of the right to be.* Her aunt said the cylinder was her mother's gift to her, Morey's birthright.

Her head was swimming. How could she and her mother be connected to the cylinder? How could something a hundred years old be her birthright? She could not make sense of this "mystery," as Katherine had deemed it. Some pieces of the puzzle were missing. She must find them. But where to look? How to start? Since professionals had tried to decipher the glyphs, she realized her e-mail to Cirrus would be of no help. She wished she hadn't sent it. If her father had maintained the cylinder was lost, he obviously had kept it secreted all these years. Perhaps he had even hidden it from his good friend Cirrus.

Morey determined she could not just sit around mulling things over. She scribbled a note for her aunt on the pad by the phone. *Gone to town. Back early afternoon.* She ripped off the piece of paper from the pad, walked to the kitchen table, slipped the paper under the cylinder.

She padded quietly out of the kitchen through the central hall and exited the Victorian. As she walked to her bike she searched the meadow across the road for signs of the two wolf dogs, hoping they'd bound out from the grassy camouflage, stretch their long sinewy bodies eager to accompany her on her trip to town, but the meadow held only the busy hum of insects up early with the sun and hard at work. She was on her own.

Morey pedaled the long hills and valleys toward town. The air was cool, light. A red- tailed hawk soared on a morning updraft. She passed no one. Island economics did not support luxury. Walking, riding horses, and bicycling were usual transportation. There was no din of people, cars, and trucks. Sounds were clear, discreet, solitary.

.At the top of the hill, she paused to study the town below. Main Street, a half-mile stretch, ended abruptly at the wharf and ferry landing. Buildings, most made of local stone, were strung along the north side of Main Street, the relatively large Apoquaque Bank the focal point. A long, clean stretch of pebbled sand and clear water ran along the south side. On the west side of Apoquaque Bank were the boating store and grocery store, on the east side the barbershop, library, and a coffee shop that doubled as the post office. It was a nice tight little town, self-sufficient, minimalist, prudent, a town that did not crave community but worshiped solitude. For the first time, she noticed that what was so common in most country towns was totally absent here on Apoquaque – churches. Her father was not an atheist but a religious outsider who practiced no formal faith and bought her up likewise, and Shelbyville Young Women's School, despite its name was anything but traditional. Yet she was surprised she had never noticed this before and found it odd in the sense of it being unusual, atypical but then Apoquaque was, if anything, idiosyncratic.

Morey looked at her watch—7:40 a.m., so too early for the library. She pedaled up to the coffee shop. On the window, black letters spelled out Mott's Coffee Shop, while underneath in smaller block was written Apoquaque Post Office.

The door opened with a jingle. A fiftyish man wearing a soda-jerk hat looked up from a griddle of pancakes. "Fred" was printed on his apron breast pocket. He eyed a petite old woman sitting at the end of the counter, then returned to his cooking. The counter formed a dogleg around the cooking area, and beyond it was an aisle that cut the back of the shop in half with three tall-backed booths on either side. Several heads appeared from the back booths, peered at Morey, and then disappeared. Straight across the room from the counter was a wall of mail slots, empty, dusty, save two with a few letters stuffed inside.

Morey chose the stool next to the storefront window and looked around. Silver and mint-green Hamilton Beach soda fountain fixtures sparkled like new. Large, round-topped Coca Cola glasses sat inside shiny metal holders. The black-and-white tile floor was immaculate. From the back booths, Morey heard muted voices. She sensed they were talking about her – the new girl in town.

The old woman studied her in silence. Then her eyes darkened, "You one of them Oilers?"

"Excuse me?"

"Oilers, work for Saturn Oil, on the rig off our shores."

Morey remembered the torn piece of paper caught in the beach grass, the headline: <u>Stop Saturn Oil.</u>

"No. I'm visiting my aunt, Katherine Chance," she replied.

The old woman's eyes widened. She put a thin finger on a small milk pitcher, slid it toward her. She poured a stream of milk into her coffee, stirred slowly, then leaned toward Morey. "Oilers, they think they own the ocean." Her voice was a soft hiss.

Fred placed a cup of coffee on the counter in front of Morey. His thick arm, covered with the fine white dust of pancake flour, drifted a thin powdery wake on the counter. He stood there, stared at her with the darkest black eyes she'd ever seen. Then she remembered: Sebastian Mott.

"Flapjack special this morning," Fred spoke loudly, tilted his cap toward a blackboard nailed into the wall: Flapjack Special, one stack, two eggs, and sausage, $2.99.

The old woman looked up from her cup of coffee, tapped her ear. "Can't hear," she mouthed, nodded toward Fred.

"Just coffee," Morey waved her hand. "I believe I met a relative. Sebastian?" She said louder, took a sip of coffee.

"Sebastian." Fred straightened up, turned, and contemplated a picture on the wall a few feet from the blackboard.

Morey followed his gaze to a framed photo. There was Sebastian, just as she remembered.

"My father, lost at sea when I was seven. Gray ghost got him."

Morey felt her jaw drop. There was some mistake. A loud click from the red and white Coca-Cola clock as its hands moved to eight o'clock made her jump, almost spilling her coffee.

She heard the old lady's low chuckle. "Eight o'clock," the old lady said. "Library opens at eight o'clock on the dot. Carmella is never late. You can count on it."

Morey looked at the old lady and wasn't sure she liked what she saw in her small, old eyes: *Yep, got you pegged. Know what you're up to. Can read your mind.* She started to get up. She needed to get out of there.

"Storm's comin' in from the south." Fred's tone was serious, his coal-black eyes zeroed in at her.

Morey almost sat back down. She made a weak attempt to smile, nodded uncomfortably. She reached in her pocket, pulled out a dollar, coffee payment, left it on the counter, turned and walked out the door.

Outside Morey stood for a moment, shook her shoulders and tried to shake off the creepiness she felt, the weird mistake about Sebastian. Apoquaque had always been a place lost in time, inhabited by eccentric people, the stuff of childhood fairytales that adult minds could not wrap themselves around. As a child, she was drawn into its upside-down world. It was special, and it made her feel special too. She had nicknamed Apoquaque. She called it Adventureland. It felt tamer, safer. But that was a long time ago. She was an adult now, and the old woman's mind reading, if that's what it was, was unsettling. And Sebastian Mott, she'd rather not go there. She looked down the street, found the small wooden building that was Apoquaque Library, grabbed her bike, and rode toward it, glad to put distance between herself and Mott's Coffee Shop.

She rested her bike against its grayed clapboard wall and walked to the library door. She opened it and felt relieved. Large windows let in a great deal of light that illuminated white, spotless walls, gracing the space with openness very different from the confining coffee shop. She could breathe in here.

Bookshelves wrapped around two back walls. The librarian's desk, front and center, had neat stacks of books and piles of papers on it. Nailed to the wall behind the desk, there was a wooden sign that looked like it had been rescued from a building demolition:

Harobed. The Believer must have Faith. A Faith that transcends the senses; if necessary defies them; defies even the power of reason.

The librarian sat at the desk, talking to a tall woman with her back to Morey. She was pale and willowy, her hair and skin thin. A tributary of blue veins stood out against each temple. The other woman moved slightly, and the librarian saw her. She looked startled.

"May I help you?"

The tall woman turned around. Thick, dark hair fell loosely around an angular, attractive face. Morey felt an instant attraction. It surprised her.

"I was wondering if you have any books on the history of Apoquaque?" Morey asked.

The librarian stiffened. "Third shelf, right of the window," she pointed, "author's Applegrate."

Morey glanced at the tall woman, who looked at Morey, a serious expression on her face. Then the tall woman turned back to the librarian. Morey felt suddenly shy. She was not used to shy.

She went to where the librarian had pointed and found the book, *A History of Apoquaque Island* by Carmella Applegrate. She flipped to the back cover. There was a picture of the author: this woman was younger, her hair darker, and she was sporting a stiff smile, but still, definitely the librarian. She wondered if others had written about Apoquaque and if Carmella only shelved her own book.

Book in hand, Morey walked the bookshelves. The library was a veritable science treasure trove. She used her fingers to count the sections - climate, oceanography, astronomy, cellular, biology, particle physics, thermodynamics. She stopped counting at the zoology section and gazed over hundreds of books dedicated to fauna representing, it seemed, every corner of the globe. She pulled out a large book, the size of an Atlas and thumbed through page upon page of intricate drawings of parrots and was reminded of Darwin's sketches of Galapagos finches. She wondered about the passion necessary to commit one's energies to such a compilation.

She heard the library door close, peered through the stacks of books to find the tall woman had left and found herself wondering what the woman had thought of her.

"Name's Hill," Carmella Applegrate said.

"Oh." Morey felt her cheeks grow warm.

"Part of a group of scientists studying our island's ecosystem," her eyes were stern, fixed on Morey.

"I'd like to take this out." Morey changed the subject, held up the book.

"Do you have a library card?"

"No, I—"

"Must have a card."

"But—"

"Read it here if you wish." She motioned to a small table and chair, went back to her work.

Morey sized up the book, two hours, no more. Before sitting she asked, "Have there been any digs on Apoquaque?"

The librarian looked at Morey as if she were crazy and shook her head no.

Inside Mott's, Hill stood by the window and looked toward the library.

"Pretty, don't ya think?" Fred said.

"Very," Hill said without turning around.

"Katherine Chance's niece, Morey," Hill heard the old lady say.

So that was it. When she'd looked at her for the first time, even when she stood with her back toward her in the library, she'd felt her presence, like something warm and good and wonderfully familiar. And still, some residue of her presence remained with her. She remembered yesterday's strong sense that something different would be added to the equation. Was that something Morey Chance? Would she become part of the work on Apoquaque? If so, she would be entering a dangerous arena. Yet, selfishly, she found herself hoping she would.

But something bothered Hill. When she met someone, even for the first time, she could tell if that person was like her. And Morey Chance was not. Yet there was something about her that made her question herself, made her wish Morey was.

15

Morey arrived back at the Victorian around five o'clock. She had spent the rest of the day in the library reading *A History of Apoquaque Island*, looking for a clue, anything connected to the cylinder, the meaning of its hieroglyphics. She found nothing.

When Morey brought her bike around to the tool shed, its doors were open, and Katherine's bike was gone. In the house, she found the cylinder where she left it on the kitchen table and next to it a note from Aunt Katherine. Katherine had gone down the road to the Bristols'. She hoped Morey didn't mind, but she'd invited some guests for dinner. If Katherine wasn't back by six, please turn the oven on, start the hens.

Morey opened the refrigerator door. Six Cornish hens, plump, seasoned, stuffed. She reasoned four guests for dinner. She had a couple of hours to kill. She looked out the window to the woods. The edge of the backyard was lined with deciduous trees - oak, maple, birch. Farther from the house, the trees became spruce, balsam, black pine, trees as familiar to her as her childhood bedroom, trees she had climbed so often she thought of them as furniture. She could pinpoint in the woods of her memory exactly where foxes had denned, where a woodpecker had hammered out his nest, the clean, round depressions where quail rested. Adventureland. The urge to explore filled her.

The kitchen screen door slapped shut behind her. Morey glanced toward the barn; it looked less sturdy than she remembered. She noticed a padlock hung from the barn door. Odd. Her eyes followed the slope of the roof down to her old rain barrel still at the barn's front left corner. She turned, walked on past the tool shed, and into the woods.

Immense old black pines towered into a cathedral of branches. Light shafted down through green needle fingers to warm blueberry, checkerberry, reindeer moss, and bunchberry below. Underfoot, soft earth and pine needles cushioned her steps. Heaven.

She saw her old path, overgrown yet still there. Black pine saplings she remembered had grown into mature trees. She looked back toward the house and caught only a swatch of white through the growth. She decided to follow the path to the tree that lived deep in the woods. Her tree, the one immortalized in the black and white photo tacked to Katherine's kitchen wall. Her gangly girl legs and long girl arms had climbed its strong limbs to a height taller than any surrounding trees. There she sat and shared her secrets, and on breezy days, her tree's needles whispered back.

She had visited the tree many times before her father forbade her to do so any longer. Something Morey had confided in him spooked him terribly. At the time, Morey hadn't understood why he had been so scared, because she had thought it simply wonderful.

One day while she was perched high atop her pine tree, a crow lighted on a branch close to her. He sat silent, intent, swaying on his perch. Large and majestic, his body shone purple. Morey reached out her skinny girl arm, stretching until her hand was inches away. Still he did not move. Then he turned his small black crow eyes upon her, lowered his head into the shroud of two raised black shoulders, and began to caw loud, repetitive, demanding caws. He glowered at her and then without so much as a sound he pushed off into air and for a hypnotic moment seemed frozen there in space like a hologram as he began the rhythmic, strobe-like beating of his wings, the rhythm so in unison with the thudding of her heart that with each wing stroke her heart pumped louder and louder until she thought her heart was going to burst from her chest.

That's when it happened, the thing that shook her father so. The crow took flight and when he did he took Morey with him. Not bodily.

Her body remained just where it was. But he took her mind with him, maybe even her soul.

Miraculously she had soared, seeing through crow eyes, gliding on crow wings, looking down through tree limbs to the forest floor. She felt no fear. It was as if this was the most natural of occurrences.

But when she ran back to tell her father, he forbade her to visit her tree or the deep woods again, or to talk of this to anyone but him or Aunt Katherine. He told her she had fallen asleep at the top of her tree and dreamed this flight. He warned her how dangerous this was, how she could have fallen, been killed. She protested vigorously, pouted for days but her father remained adamant. No more woods until she promised not to journey deep into them and, above all, never to visit her tree. She had broken her promise only once. To say good-bye.

A wind pushed through the trees and the air filled with the smell of balsam. A shadow fell over the forest and Morey looked up into dark clouds. Mott's storm. It had come suddenly, eclipsing the light, chilling the air. In the dimness, things looked spectral, macabre. She felt alone, too far from the house, jittery. Better start back.

She shivered, caught by her own internal state as much as the impending storm, rubbed the goose bumps from her arms. She had not gotten far when she heard something snap. She jumped involuntarily, turned in the direction of the noise, and heard it. Panting. Nothing out of breath. Slow. Rhythmical. Steady. Animal. A small cloud of breath hung, pumping slowly, condensed by the cold.

Then they opened slowly, or turned to catch the dim light, yellow eyes like glistening gold. She took a step, and a second pair of eyes caught light. Ghostly, bodiless in the dark brush, both sets of eyes hung suspended a few feet from the ground - the height of - wolf-dogs. The thought calmed her somewhat. Then both sets of eyes blinked in a slow sleepy manner as if signaling assent.

Morey walked the woods back toward the house without seeing them again, but she felt the wolf-dogs' presence every step of the way. She tried to remember what was becoming increasingly further from her consciousness: the feeling of normalcy.

16

John Feuer parked his car at the road's curve and stood with his binoculars, waiting. He watched as Katherine Chance rode her bike down the driveway and turned onto the road away from him. He saw Morey disappear into the woods. He waited till she was out of sight, then threw the binoculars onto the passenger seat and opened his iPhone. He punched out an e-mail.

Dear Ms. Chance,
I examined the photograph of your cylinder closely. I am sorry, but it is of no interest. I believe what you have is a replica, nothing origi-nal. The hieroglyphics bear no resemblance to actual ancient symbols on the Buttu Highlands artifact.
Sorry to disappoint.
Sincerely,
Rupert Cirrus

He hit send. Using *Predator*, he had captured Morey's e-mail to Cirrus before it arrived. He needed to respond to it, tidy up loose ends.

He left the car and headed down the road to the Victorian. Within minutes, he was walking up the gravel driveway.

He found the front door unlocked and was disappointed. He was good at what he did, loved the rush it gave him, hated when people made things easy. He looked at his watch. He had decided to give him-self ten minutes to search the house. No more. He had no way of know-ing when either woman would be back. He moved his hand inside his jacket onto the butt of his gun, which sat firmly in its shoulder holster. He gave the gun a tap, part of a ritual he enjoyed. Protocol was for children, nothing but simple logic after all. But liturgy protected. Liturgy gave him power.

He entered the house.

His gaze went right to the central stairs. He would start upstairs, work his way down. If either returned while he was still in the house, he wanted to be close to the first floor, get off a clean shot, get out quickly. He took the stairs two at a time, stopped at the second floor landing, counted the rooms, decided this floor would take him three minutes. Then he bounded up the spiral staircase.

It did not take him long to finish the tower room and second floor - five minutes to be exact. The library and dining room took an additional three. He entered the kitchen, was surprised to see the cylinder sitting nice and pretty on the kitchen table. He walked over to it, took out his iPhone and opened up its scanning device, a nifty application loaded by the NSA. He punched in a code and moved it to within two inches of the cylinder. Immediately a hologram of the cylinder appeared on the screen. Interestingly, the cylinder appeared hollow.

He waited till the hologram pulsed yellow, indicating the scanning device had finished analyzing every molecule. He punched in another code, sent the data to Graham and waited.

A message came back.

Valuable but not what we want. Leave it. Keep looking.

He walked into the central hall, stood in front of the grandfather clock, opened it, reached inside, and stopped the pendulum. He ran his hands up and down the wood walls. Nothing. He gave the pendulum a push, watched it swing back. He closed the glass door and glanced at his watch. He had methodically searched the house, leaving everything exactly as he found it. One minute remaining. He did not want to leave empty-handed.

That's when he sensed something. Something watching him. He glanced around the central hall, saw nothing. He felt the hairs on the back of his neck rising the way they had when he was a kid at the thud of his stepfather's beer bottle on the kitchen table, the signature of a small, hollow man who took pleasure in spitting on him, punching him, breaking his bones until the night he fought back, older and stronger, and killed him. He moved his hand to his holster, unlatched it and started backing toward the front door, scanning around him.

His eyes registered it. His mind took a moment more. A huge black crow perched on the banister at the top of the stairs stared down at him. He swung his head back to the front door, still closed. Crazy old lady kept a crow in the house. He shook off the creepy feeling, looked at his watch. *Time to go.* He raised his gaze just as the large dark body soared straight down at him. He ducked, but not quickly enough. He felt a sharp pain at his right temple. Huge black wings beat inches from his head, deafening caws echoed in his ears. He raised his arms, tried to cover his head. Almost stumbling, he made his way to the front door, opened it and pushed his body out.

He stopped on the porch. His head smarted. He put his fingers to his forehead and brought them down. Blood.

Fucking crow. He wanted to go back into the house. He needed just one shot to blast the crow into a mass of feathers and blood.

But his time was up. *Later*, he thought.

17

Candlelight flickered through the Victorian's windows. A shadow moved within the dining room stopping Morey in her tracks. She heard the murmur of voices. Company. She'd lost track of the time. She looked down at her jeans and sneakers, the leaf caught in her shoe laces. Not dinner attire.

She raced up the porch steps, slipped through the front door, and closed it quietly behind her. She distinguished two baritones and a woman's light voice, not her aunt's, coming from the kitchen. She glanced at the grandfather clock. Quarter to seven. She'd have time for a fast shower. She padded up the stairs. The voices stopped suddenly just as she reached the landing freezing her in her tracks like a skittish feral cat on alert. She waited till the voices rose again, then raced the rest of the way to the tower room.

The shower's watery needles soothed her tired muscles, not used to miles of biking hilly terrain. She put her face directly under the showerhead and let the water wash through her hair, down her body and pool around her feet on the shower floor. The cleansing water renewed her, gave her the resolve to face this evening's company. She quickly dried herself, then rifled through her luggage. She found the green-gray silk summer dress that she had had no intention of packing, but had thrown in at the last moment. She slipped into it. She rubbed her hair vigorously with a towel until it was dry enough, ran a comb through it, and tossed it with her fingers. She looked at herself in the mirror. She was satisfied she wouldn't embarrass her aunt.

Surprisingly, she found herself thinking of the woman in the library. Of course, she'd found women attractive before, but this draw was different. It puzzled and intrigued her. It was like the moment you see someone and it stops you. Just stops you and for a long moment you study this person and think: Who is this? Because it feels somehow important, critical that you pay attention. Take heed. The world has stopped to show you someone.

She hadn't had much luck in love. She knew the women in her life would say it was because she had a bit of an attitude problem. There was that vague, kiss-of-death label - distant. Some women confused her distance as a challenge, found it provocative. The problem was it eventually, always led to a struggle they couldn't win. Realizing this - soon, always - they walked away. She was never disappointed.

The women she'd dated had been intelligent, had good senses of humor. She'd found them interesting, enjoyed the sexual thrill of new relationships but what followed lacked intimacy. There was always some barrier to the kind of union she wanted. She knew in her heart it was because of her inability to connect, her inexplicable sense of separateness.

She preferred to think of herself as independent, self-reliant, free-willed. She knew that if she'd the courage to lie on the shrink's couch, the analysis would be this: that she felt not only abandoned by her father, but illogical as it might be, by her dead mother as well. Consequently, she lacked faith in other people. Her vow never to need anyone grew stronger with each year of her lonely childhood till she became steeled with an abiding faith in herself alone. But she knew also it was about control. She had developed a tight-fisted need for it. Not control over anybody else but control of herself, as if demons would fly out of her if she let down her guard.

Laughter rose from downstairs. She took one last glance at herself in the mirror, turned, and left the tower room. She descended the staircase and followed the voices into the dining room. Three guests were seated at the table, her aunt at the head. The two chairs closest to Katherine were empty.

Katherine looked up as she entered, gave her a quizzical what-have-you-been up-to look, and then waved for Morey to take the chair on her left, waited till she was seated.

"Morey, let me introduce my dearest friends."

Katherine began with Herman Bristol seated next to Morey.

"A pleasure," Herman gently pumped her hand. Salt-and-pepper hair and deep laugh lines suggested he was in his sixties. Clear, intelligent, hazel eyes shone through a pair of wire-rimmed glasses. He wore a thick, cream-colored Irish sweater with suede elbow patches. Underneath, a slightly frayed but ironed collar closed by a plaid green bow tie gave him the look of an eccentric college professor, Morey saw a little of her father in him.

"Herman is a geologic engineer," Katherine said. "He has, however, resigned from his position with Saturn Oil," there was approval in Katherine's voice. "Ethel is my best friend and confidante and Herman's wife," Katherine motioned to a woman seated across from Herman. "Ethel is editor-in-chief, sole journalist and printer for our island's only newspaper, *The Apoquaque Free Press.*"

In her mind, Morey saw the scrap of old newspaper caught in beach grass, the headline: <u>Stop Saturn Oil</u>.

"I've so admired your work," Ethel purred. She was not a pretty woman. She had a large lumpy nose and unruly, blond-gray hair. Albert Einstein's sister came to mind. "Perhaps you'd do a spread in the *Free Press,* photos of Apoquaque, of course." There was a child-like quality of delight emanating from her, in particular from her small, glimmering sapphire eyes.

Morey smiled, nodded.

Katherine turned last to a large man seated at the head of the table furthest from Katherine. His massive bulk and substantial height made him look out of his element at the elegantly set dinner table.

"This gentleman is Charlie Dancer.

"Fisherman par excellence," Ethel added proudly.

"Well now, I don't know about that." Morey thought she saw a faint blush. "This island's raised many a better fisherman."

"Nonsense," Ethel protested. "Charlie can translate the cries of the gulls, the whispers of the winds," She looked directly at Morey, held her gaze so intently that Morey dropped hers.

Charlie rose and extended a big, weathered hand. Thick fingers and a paw with the feel of a rough-skinned melon eclipsed Morey's hand. He pumped her hand gently.

"Our fourth guest has been detained," Katherine nodded toward the table setting directly across from Morey. "Hopefully, she will make it for dessert."

"Or not at all, most likely," Ethel huffed then caught herself and looked sheepishly at Katherine. "Well, yes then, good food, fine wine, dear friends. Let the evening begin," she recouped.

And so it began. The company dug into Katherine's scrumptious fare, drank bottle after bottle of wine. Morey felt she'd dropped back in time to a medieval feast with Aunt Katherine as the monarch. The conversation was alive and easy. Charlie spoke lovingly of Apoquaque, the freedom of life as a fisherman. Herman spoke of the ethical dilemma that led to his resignation from Saturn Oil, how despite his voluminous proofs and admonitions, the company had decided to drill for oil off Apoquaque's shores, so dangerously close to an oceanic fault line. *Oilers*, Morey remembered.

Ethel lectured passionately about mankind's blind disregard for the Earth's other inhabitants, its selfish invasion of the last stands of wilderness.

Morey found comfort in the like-mindedness of her aunt's friends whom she was quickly coming to know as people of conscience. She felt buoyed by the ebb and flow of their conversation. Time seemed to slow in a lazy, drugged way. She thought she'd better relax on the wine.

"So Morey, do you have any friends on the island from your summers here?" Ethel asked.

"No." Morey looked down at her plate, suddenly self-conscious of her lifelong theme of self-imposed isolation. "Unless you call two wolf-dogs friends," she added trying to make light of her lack of connectedness to the human race.

Ethel raised an eyebrow, "Wolf-dogs?"

Herman moaned. "Now Ethel, don't get started."

"Shush," Ethel fluttered her hand dismissively in the air, zeroed in on Morey. "Morey dear, what do you mean wolf-dogs?"

Morey looked around the table. No one made eye contact save Ethel.

"I met two wild dogs at the pier the day I arrived. They followed me to just about the front door then disappeared into the field across from the house. And today, I swear I saw them in the woods." Morey felt a kind of unease like when you get the feeling you are the only one who doesn't know what everyone else knows.

"Two sightings – very, very impressive, my dear."

"You know them?"

Herman moaned again.

"A pair of wolf-dogs is legendary here," Katherine raised her glass, swirled the red wine ever so slowly against the curved side and drained her glass.

"Herman, we need more wine," Ethel glared at Herman. She waited till he left the room and then leaned in toward Morey. "There are many stories about these wolf-dogs, stories of sightings, sometimes mere glimpses or simply the echoes of distant howling. There's the story of Richard Littleworth that Old Man Littleworth swears by to this day," Ethel's eyes gleamed. "When the elder Littleworth was a young father and Richard just six years old, they went out fishing. A squall came up out of nowhere, the way they do around here, and capsized the boat. Tragically, little Richard was swept away. For days, everyone with a boat searched the waters. Everyone on the island combed the beaches. Then very late one night, after all hope was lost—"

"Don't forget to tell Morey these stories are older than you are." Herman stepped into the room, placed two bottles of Australian Shiraz on the table. "That would make them the oldest living dogs on the planet." He pulled a corkscrew from his pocket and went to work on one bottle.

Ethel feigned annoyance, took a breath, and continued. "Late one night, Littleworth was awakened by strange sounds. Hauntingly sad howlings like the calls of wolves. Compelled to follow these sirens, he stepped into the night. Barefoot, in his nightclothes, he walked through the fields and into the forest. The night was black, moonless and when the wolves' voices ceased, Littleworth stood lost in the depths of the forest. That's when he saw them for the first time."

Ethel reached for the newly opened bottled, poured a refill, and swallowed heartedly never once dropping her gaze from Morey.

"Them?" Morey said, her voice hushed.

"Two dark figures, shadows moving through the underbrush, swift phantoms on the hunt. A sense of purpose, an urgency filled Littleworth. Bare feet bruised and bleeding, brambles catching and ripping at his clothes, his skin, he ran with the shadow dogs. He felt euphoric. He had no idea how long or in what direction they ran. Forest cleared to brush. Brush cleared to beach," Ethel's voice had become almost breathless, "his bruised feet thankful for the cool damp sand, he realized he was running alone straight toward three faint figures ahead on the beach. He stopped, couldn't believe his eyes. Right there in front of him sat the two wolf-dogs. And between them was young Richard, chilled to the bone but perfectly fine," Ethel smiled contently, sat back in her chair.

"Amazing," Morey said.

"There's more," Charlie glanced at Herman.

Herman shrugged. "Go on."

"Many islanders have seen the dogs for a brief moment," Charlie added. "Then they disappear like ghosts, only to reappear some distance away."

"Always leaving them with a feeling of being beckoned," Ethel interrupted, "compelled to follow, and inevitably being led to some person or animal needing help."

"Millicent Weeks," Charlie continued, "eight years old, fell down an abandoned well. Her ten-year-old brother reported two wolves led him straight to the well. Phineas Seitz, lives alone, fell off his tractor and broke his leg. Lay out there for two days before Bess Frelove, out riding, saw two dogs in the distance and decided to track them. Almost ran right over poor Phineas. There have been beached turtles and whales, injured seals."

"Seems any time something gets rescued, this old yarn begins again," Herman grumbled.

"The story of the wolf-dogs dates to the days pirates were active on our seas," Katherine added. "The legend begins with a terrible storm that sank the vessel, The Charles, off Apoquaque. The only survivors to make it to shore were these two dogs. One dog was grievously injured, her body smashed badly against the rocks by the raging surf. When the storm subsided, an islander found them on the beach. The injured one had died. Try as he might, the man could not get the other dog to leave his dead friend. Taking pity on the poor scrawny creature, who could not survive much longer without food and shelter, the islander picked up the body of the dead dog and brought them both to Albertina Mae Hettie."

"Albertina is herself legendary," Ethel chimed in, "she served way back then as island nurse and doctor."

"More witch doctor than anything else," Herman huffed.

"When Albertina was left alone with the two dogs," Katherine continued, "the living dog spoke to her, and said, 'If you help my friend, we promise to keep a contract with you.' So Albertina sang over the dead dog's body, moved her hands over the broken carcass. She sang for hours and hours, and the living dog joined her howling a melancholy prayer. Their two voices folded around one another, caressed the lifeless body, healed its broken bones and breathed life back into it." Katherine finished, sat back in her chair.

Morey felt herself shiver involuntarily. The hairs on her arms rose, as if lightening had stuck nearby. "My God, what a story," Morey reached for the Shiraz, refilled her glass. She sipped her wine, feeling again that growing sense of undefined unease. Ethel's small sapphire eyes seemed to entreat her, her face petitioned Morey to react. "The contract?" she asked, her voice sounding small.

Ethel looked pleased. "A promise that the two dogs would never leave Apoquaque," Ethel's voice was low, hushed as if she were revealing an ancient secret, "that they would protect her and the island's inhabitants, human and animal alike for all time."

There was a knock at the front door. Ethel jumped and spilled her wine. "My goodness," she patted the table with her napkin.

Herman rolled his eyes. "I'll get it." He left for the front door.

Morey's back was to the entrance of the dining room, but the glass door of the china cabinet in front of her caught the guest's reflection.

For the first time in her life, as far as she could remember, she felt totally unnerved. Standing just a few feet from her was the woman from the library.

"Morey, I'd like you to meet Hill," Herman said. "She and I are working together to protect Apoquaque's fragile ecosystem."

Morey instantly understood the meaning of the phrase 'the world fell away,' for hers faded away at lightning speed. Sights and sounds receded, became meaningless as if the tangible world dissolved. Her only awareness was she and Hill. The only motion was her body turning through what felt like molasses to face her. The only sound her thin, "Glad to meet you." She felt totally adolescent.

Morey heard her aunt clear her throat and watched her straighten in her chair. Morey felt the message implicitly: get a grip.

"The pleasure is all mine." All poise, Hill seemed not to notice Morey's infatuation. She placed two Firestone merlots on the table in front of Katherine. "I hope I'm not too late with these."

"Never too late for merlot," Ethel cheered.

Hill took the empty seat across from Morey. Herman poured her a glass of wine, and conversation thankfully turned to mundane things. Marvis, the postmaster, was taking a vacation, her first in twenty-five years. Jerome Appleward bought Littleworth's old tractor. Pheebe Mountain caught a thousand-pound blue fin tuna. Throughout it all, Morey lost no awareness of the woman across from her. Hill's face lit by flickering candlelight, she did not comment on the price of tractors or vacations. She remained intent, quiet. Despite this, Morey couldn't help but think Hill must feel some draw to her too. How could something so strong be one-sided?

When dessert came Hill declined, stood, and asked if anyone would like to join her outside on the porch. When no one else replied, Morey said she would.

"Show Hill your cylinder," Ethel said.

Morey noticed Katherine shoot Ethel a look.

"When I visited Ethel and Herman this afternoon," Katherine said, "I told them about your mother's gift. I hope you don't mind."

"On the contrary, I need all the help I can get."

"Don't know anything about such cylinders," Ethel sputtered, her fingers toying with her napkin.

Hill glanced at Katherine, looked like a woman who had suddenly figured something out. "May I have a look at it?" Hill asked.

18

Morey walked out onto the porch, the cylinder in her hand. Hill stood alone, her hands braced on the railing, leaning out toward the sky. Two glasses of wine were balanced on the railing next to her. She turned and smiled at Morey. Then her gaze dropped to the cylinder. "May I?" She extended her hand.

Morey walked over and placed the cylinder in Hill's hand.

"Interesting," Hill turned it over. "Ah, yes," she gave it back to Morey. "I believe what you have here is something very valuable," her gray-green eyes locked with Morey's.

"Really." Morey no longer cared about the mysterious cylinder. What was the matter with her? She put the cylinder down on the railing between them, took a step back. She needed some distance.

Hill turned away from her, leaned out over the railing into the night. "Have you been having strange dreams?"

"Why yes. How did you—"

"Dreams are associated with these cylinders, all kinds of dreams. It is said that if the cylinder is not in the hands of the rightful person, the cylinder will find that person through the power of dreams. Both rightful owner and the possessor will be haunted until the cylinder is united with the person it is meant for. Then the new dreams begin."

"I received the cylinder yesterday," Morey's voice rose, "and the dream that's been haunting me, well, last night was the first night I didn't have that dream but dreamt another," the words tumbled out of her the way confidences rush out between two best friends. Morey felt suddenly silly, childish. "What do you mean the rightful owner?" She tried to sound level-headed, adult.

"The cylinders are handed down mother to daughter. There's usually something inside - a symbolic guidepost of a quest."

"Quest?"

"Something the daughter must learn. An initiation, a rite of passage that if accomplished successfully will mean the daughter receives a new cylinder, a very different cylinder that is purported to have powers."

"Powers, something inside," Morey mused. "There is a thin line, like a seam. I've tried but I can't find a way of opening it." Morey was about to pick it up when something stopped her, something internal, something intuitive. *Use your mind, Morey. Make it open.* She heard it as if in a faraway land, this voice somehow not unknown to her.

Reflected light from inside the house made the cylinder seem luminescent. Squinting, her eyes barely open, she stared at the cylinder, told herself to concentrate. She narrowed her thoughts till they became focused tight as a laser beam. Then with one mental push, she told the cylinder to open. Gracefully, like a clam revealing a pearl, the cylinder split open.

Morey moved to the porch railing, looked down at the opened cylinder. Inside was a necklace.

She reached in, gently removed the necklace, and held it up to the porch light. "Incredible," she said softly.

"How did you get it to open?" Hill asked.

"I'm not sure I did." She studied her mother's gift. The chain was a continuous strand of smooth dark purple stone - at least it appeared to be stone, felt like stone, yet it was as flexible as string. There was no latch. Hanging from the unbroken circle was a pendant made of the same purplish-black material.

"It's a sea lion," Morey held the pendant between her thumb and forefinger. "Whiskers, ears etched on its face, but no eyes. Strange."

"May I?" Hill held out her hand.

Hill took the necklace from her, slid it over Morey's head, and as she did, Hill's hand lightly touched Morey's neck, and from that point, a luscious warmth radiated outward across her skin, then inside her. She felt Hill's eyes studying her; she looked down at the porch floor.

"I may know this little sea lion," Hill said.

"How could you possibly?" she half-laughed.

The screen door squeaked open, startling Morey.

"Are you disappointed in your mother's gift?" Katherine stood with her hand holding open the porch door.

"No, it's beautiful." Her hand rose, her fingers touched the pendant, hovered about it, unable to resist it.

Morey saw the others behind Katherine, Ethel's neck craning. She wondered how long they had been there, watching. Then unexpectedly, she was overwhelmed by the conviction that what had happened just now on the porch had been meant to happen, that the group had expected this, perhaps even planned for it. It chilled her.

"I propose a toast!" Ethel pushed the group onto the porch, raised her glass, her gaze summoning the others to do the same. Caught in Ethel's command, Morey picked up hers. When everyone's glass was lifted, Ethel's voice rose. "To Morey's heritage," Ethel raised her glass to her lips, drank thirstily.

Ill at ease, Morey lifted the glass to her lips but did not drink. Looking around at this odd group of people, she could not shake the eeriness she felt. She sensed something else too, something from the past, something that had always been there, dormant, waiting, whispering for its freedom.

Morey was glad everyone had left. Her mind was muddled, mixed with the stories she heard tonight, her attraction to Hill, and the bizarre coincidence that Hill had knowledge about her cylinder. Strangely, she wished her father were here. He'd been so analytical, could figure out the most puzzling things with his straightforward logic. She curled into the window seat. Resting her arm against her chest, she held the purple sea lion tight in the palm of her hand. The little pendant felt warm. She leaned her head against the cool windowpane, watched dark clouds skim past the moon. Soft raindrops hit the window. She tumbled into a deep sleep.

Blackness enveloped her - dark, immense, infinite. A brilliant moon hung in a sky so huge she could not take it all in. Exhaustion streamed through her body. *Her arms driven beat rhythmically against the air. Below her stretched an immense pool of shimmering, dark water. She was flying over the ocean. Her wings pushed persistently against the wildly churning roller coaster of the wind. Her journey had a predetermined destination. A compelling inner drive for survival made her navigating instinctual. She and her companions rode the front line of Mott's storm. A call issued from her throat, immediately echoed by what must have been a hundred birds. Some voices far behind, barely audible, friends, falling behind, swallowed by the storm. Faster, push harder. Stay ahead of the storm.*

A large opaque hole opened on the reflective sea, a black oblique surface dotted with pinpoints of light. Home! Excited cries echoed the news through the flock, their numbers not as rich as before. Excitement edged with exhaustion and hunger melted into sadness for the loss of companions.

Freefall toward land. Pinpoints of light became street lights, illuminated windows of houses. The flock broke up, headed for distinct parts of the island. She flew away from the lights toward the darkness of land, her home - fields and meadows lit solely by the moon and stars. The journey's end meant safety for another season.

Renewed strength overcame exhaustion and every swirl and swoop became joy. Tuck the wing slightly. Down on the tail. Natural, effortless, exquisite flight.

Things that had been miniaturized grew to true size. Ahead was the Victorian. She saw herself, Morey, asleep, curled in the window seat. She flew past the window, sailed over Katherine's garden, landed in the spruce tree. Heavy rain would follow soon. Shelter was essential.

She chose a branch close to the trunk where overlapping branches knit a needle roof. She knew this tree well. This branch. Fluffing out her feathers to produce a pocket of warmth, her feet clutched the branch tightly and the tips of her talons broke through the brittle bark into the wood beneath. A piece flaked off, fell long and silently down.

Then she was there. At the forest floor, running, paws pushing harder, rhythmically on the worn earth. Brush cracked as she hurdled windfalls in ancient woods dense with undergrowth. Pungent scents filled her nostrils, air thick with delicious musk, acrid animal urine, the clean smell of wet, decaying wood. Whiffs traveled from miles away. Hints of long ago tainted the air, soaked the soil. Running in a delicious river of odors, she knew every aspect, every stick, each shape. A thin line to the right, nearly indistinguishable in the brush, was a fox path. Last night, a few yards into the path, the fox had stopped to finish his meal of grouse. The small disturbance in the leaves, a mounding ahead hid a rabbit, eyes glistening, muscles taut ready to spring.

She listened to the sound of her own panting and felt the most curious and unsettling sensation of movement within, of a turning in her heart and mind toward a new point on the compass.

19

A sharp chest pain woke Francis Chance. He took in a gulp of air like he'd been held underwater and opened his eyes. The first thing he saw was the ceiling. It was low with a track of small lights. His gaze followed the ceiling to the left where it curved into a metal wall. He turned his head. It was night. His own distorted reflection stared back from what could only be an airplane window. His body felt like lead, yet his mind was clear. Crystal clear.

"Lazarus awakes!" A shadow bent over him, and he felt his back moving upright. "Time to sit up, pretty amazing these seats, recline into a bed." The man plopped down heavily in the seat next to him. A faint smell of perspiration rose from his clothes.

Francis remembered, remembered Feuer coming right at him, the hot stick at his neck, his tumbling. A current of anxiety ran through him. "Am I - did I?" The words came out in a rasp. His throat burned, and each breath had an unpleasant, metallic taste.

"Die? No, not really, been on ice for a few weeks, needed to wait till the funeral was over. You're very much alive."

Francis tried to move, and then realized his arms were restrained by straps.

"A precaution. If you're a good boy, they'll come off."

"Who the bloody hell are you?" he croaked. He used his elbows to raise himself up, felt the pins and needles of blood moving into muscle. "What funeral?"

"Amazing how lucid one wakes from this drug. Orders were not to affect your mind. Looks like the little concoction worked." The man unlatched Francis's seat's armrest, pulled out a table, swung it in front of him, then placed a laptop on it. He punched some keys and moved the screen toward Francis.

There in bold type were the death notices from the *Maine Chronicle*. His gaze swung down the page.

Chance, Francis, PhD. Professor of Archeology at Braddard College, Maine. Survived by daughter, Memory Chance, and cousin, Katherine Chance.

Francis was horrified. He heard the man chuckling as if enjoying some demented game at his expense.

"That answers the funeral question. As for who am I? Name's Stanley Protsky," the man straightened up in his seat. "PhD, Physics, Harvard. I'm here to catch Sleeping Beauty up." Protsky hit some keys on the computer. "Let's start here."

Francis looked at the screen and began reading his daughter's e-mail to Rupert Cirrus. It pained him that she thought he was dead. It terrified him that they were watching her and knew she had the cylinder. His only thought was that he must somehow protect her.

"What is this about? What do you want?"

"About?" Protsky looked at him with a quizzical smile. "About?" he said louder, a hint of annoyance in his tone. "What your whole life's been about. The reason you mastered Ethipic, Sanskrit, Zend, Pahlevi, Arabic, Syrian, Chaldean, Persian, etcetera, etcetera to decipher the ancient script, to crack the hieroglyphics. This is about decoding the cylinder."

Francis felt it inside of him then. A small laugh. A sharp, piercing snicker at the absurdity of Protsky's statement. "The cylinder can't be deciphered," Francis glared at him.

"You'd better hoped it can," Protsky snapped.

"Listen, you can't hold me. It's against my rights." Francis tried to stay calm. His throat felt like he had eaten broken glass.

"Dead men don't have rights." Protsky closed out the e-mail and opened another window. "Now," Protsky began, "let's get you up to speed." He keyed in a password. "Pay attention. I don't like to repeat myself." He was all business, cared little for the emotional kick in the stomach Francis might be feeling. "My work concerns amazing phenomena. Phenomena I'm only now beginning to understand, anomalies in the Earth's electromagnetic and gravitational fields that appear above a specific location, never to be repeated there again. The government considers my work critical, pulled out all the stops, given me access to classified information that would make your hair stand on end." Protsky looked smug.

Francis tried to think. His mind was reeling, spinning back to one thought - Morey. They'd intercepted her e-mail. They knew she had the cylinder. Had Feuer paid her the same sort of visit?

"We have another one." Protsky broke his racing thoughts.

"What?"

"Logically, a good daddy is wondering about his daughter and of course, the cylinder. We have another cylinder. Plans now are to use the one we have," Protsky sighed, apparently impatient with this explanatory detour.

"My daughter, she's safe, right?" He felt like a POW begging for a scrap of food.

"OK, let's get this sentimental part out of the way so we can get down to business. When Feuer paid you a visit in your office at Braddard, he questioned you about the cylinder."

Francis remembered his relief that he'd gotten rid of the cylinder, mailed it to Katherine.

"Feuer was toying with you, like a cat with a caught bird it has no need for, other than the sheer enjoyment of watching its futile, suffering dance. We had already tracked your little package to Apoquaque. Feuer knew this, just wanted to have a little extra fun. He can be a loose cannon, a rogue, follows instructions but always adds his own signature."

"My daughter, she's safe?" Francis mustered his strongest voice.

"We have Feuer on Apoquaque keeping a close watch on her. So the question you need to ask is not whether your daughter is safe, but how do you keep your daughter safe?"

20

Morey stood in the kitchen wrapped in an ankle-length bathrobe she'd found hanging on a hook on the back of the bathroom door. Opened wide at the neck, the robe fell loosely around her shoulders. She poured her first cup of coffee, sipped it slowly. She put the cup down, ran her fingers through hair wet from her morning shower, pushed it away from her face. It occurred to her she felt fully rested. The constant fatigue brought on by night after night of fitful sleep was gone, gone with her anxiety-producing dream.

Hill said these cylinders were associated with dreams, haunted the proper owner, called to them until they were united. She remembered the beautiful dream of flight she had last night, so vivid. Her hand rose and her fingers found the sea lion pendant. *United,* she thought.

She walked to her aunt's laptop. It was on. She checked for e-mail. Cirrus had sent a reply. She opened it and read it.

Curious, so brief and blunt, nothing like Cirrus. He was always so warm and welcoming. Death makes people behave strangely, feel so uncomfortable they seek distance from those who are grieving. It was better this way. Things were becoming a bit confusing. The fewer people involved the better.

She padded softly through the central hall toward the library, careful not to wake Katherine. Tall mahogany sliders dwarfed her. She pushed apart the heavy doors, drew a breath of library air - old leather and dust. She walked over to the small fireplace framed by local stone and glided her hand over the cool granite mantle. Above it hung a large mirror. The glass, aged and smoky colored, appeared to possess more depth than reflection. Two wingback chairs flanked the fireplace, a small round marble-topped table at each. Crowded bookshelves rose from floor to ceiling on each side of the fireplace and along an adjacent wall. A heavy, ornately carved desk positioned at an angle on a huge oriental carpet faced the walls of leather-covered books.

Morey browsed the titles. There were nautical books, pirate lore, classics, history and philosophy collections, poetry, gardening and cooking books, an astronomy and geology section, all just as she remembered. She stopped in front of her father's collection: archeology and anthropology books that took up several shelves, all left behind that night she and her father left Apoquaque. She moved her finger across titles, down backs of leather-bound spines. Her hand stopped on something rougher than a bound book. She pulled it from the shelf. It was a manuscript.

Homo occultus, by Francis Chance.

"One can learn a great deal about a person by observing her bookshelves," Katherine said, startling her. She had appeared in the doorway without Morey hearing her approach. "As one can by observing what she takes from the shelves." She walked to Morey's side. "I see you've chosen from your father's collection."

Morey smiled faintly. "Have you read it?"

"I've read every book on these shelves, some twice, Apoquaque's winters fire up the literary spirit. But your father's manuscript, no. However," she paused as if searching for the right way to say this, "he did discuss it with me."

Morey looked at the manuscript in her hand. "Can you tell me about it?" She didn't know why, but she felt uncomfortable, as if she was prying, as if she'd unlocked Katherine's private safe without permission and reached inside. She handed the manuscript over to Katherine like someone who'd gotten caught eating the last piece of pie, fork en route to the mouth, pie plate in hand.

"This manuscript is your father's thesis written after your birth, never presented." Katherine inspected it closely. "Interesting you chose this." She walked over to one of the burgundy-upholstered wingback chairs, sat down, and rested the manuscript on her lap, her hands folded over it. She stared blindly at the manuscript for a moment, apparently searching her memory, and then looked up. Morey caught the message in her eyes: sit down next to me, pay attention.

Morey took the seat across from her.

"Your father's thesis," Katherine began, "discusses peoples that are very old. Cultures that have changed little even under the sharp light and pressures of modern day, much like the Aborigines of Australia, the Bushmen of Africa, and the tribes deep within the Amazon. First People, your father called them," Katherine paused, looked deep in thought as if she were contemplating how to go on. "Your father proposed a theory that another group of First People existed, an undiscovered group. Ancient, similar to all First People in that they were not driven by a need to accumulate wealth, power, prestige, they were people living in harmony with their environment. But this undiscovered group was unlike any people that ever existed, past or present. Your father postulated that they walk among us but are invisible to us."

"Invisible people," Morey smiled.

"Not literally invisible." Katherine moved in her chair as if realizing the explanation would be difficult. "Your father believed that in order to survive and accomplish their cultural imperatives, this group assimilated into the other peoples of the world, effectively cloaking themselves. They became Asians, Europeans, Africans, but they were not. You would never know they were different," she paused, "unless you were one of them." Her voice had a catch in it, as if the words were difficult to speak. She looked as if she were reliving a disturbing memory. Her eyes were distant, and her face suddenly looked weary. She stirred in her chair again, as if she had just remembered she was there. "They walk among us, but we do not see them for who they truly are."

Morey digested it all in silence. "Doesn't sound like Dad," she said.

"You know, of course, the meaning of the word *hominids*."

Morey nodded. She was the daughter of an archeologist after all. "The word refers to all of the primates on our family tree, including Homo sapiens."

"Your father must have taught you the basic history of human evolution."

"Sure."

"Tell me what he taught you about the Neanderthals and the first Homo sapiens."

Morey thought for a moment. "Scientists first thought the Neanderthals were the ancestors of Homo sapiens. Later evidence showed both existed at the same time. Two branches of the same evolutionary tree. Both hominids. The Neanderthals died out, and Homo sapiens alone spread across the earth."

"Good," Katherine sounded pleased. "Now what if I told you Homo sapiens were not alone?"

"I'd ask you to explain."

"After the Neanderthals became extinct, around the time when Homo sapiens were creating cave art, your father believed man took yet another evolutionary leap – a tiny change in genes to a more evolved human. He named the evolved ones *Homo occultus*."

"Hidden man."

"Correct. Like the Neanderthals and Homo sapiens before them, Homo sapiens and this new form of human, Homo occultus, now inhabited the planet together. Two branches of the same evolutionary tree."

"Both hominids."

"Very good."

"What happened to Homo occultus?"

"Nothing. Your father believed they are still here today."

"Still here but hidden from us," she half-laughed. "The First People who cloak themselves. I didn't know Dad wrote science fiction."

"As I've said, this was your father's thesis, which he never presented." Her tone was curt.

"I would hope he never presented it. Weren't things bad enough? Wasn't his reputation already in the shitter?" Her tone was hard, laced with the memory of childhood shame. She stopped herself when she saw the don't-go-there look on Katherine's face. "OK, I'll play. Let's say Dad did believe this fantasy. Why did these people hide?"

"Many reasons, first was survival. Man's history is replete with superstition, fear, and destruction of anything different. Homo occultus were not conquerors, destroyers. They did not wage war. It was not in them. They were warriors of a different kind. This put them at a distinct disadvantage. For centuries, they hid in the wilderness. When the wilderness diminished, they came out cloaked as Homo sapiens."

"Pretending to be Homo sapiens, but they weren't. Plus they were more evolved." Something intuitive didn't want to play this game anymore but her curiosity was piqued. "More evolved, how?"

Katherine got that faraway look in her eyes, and then her eyes cleared. She turned her head, leveled her gaze at Morey. "Aptitudes, abilities they possess."

Morey got that weird feeling you get when you're getting scared and you want to scream and turn tail and run, but you like the exciting, creepy feeling too much. "I'll bite. What abilities?" she asked.

Katherine brought her voice low. "These people called it magic."

The word hit her in the stomach. *She has the magic.* Her dream flashed through her neural circuitry. She had to stop her arms from rising up, her hands from covering her ears like in the dream. There it was again, that suffocating feeling, the need to gasp for air.

"You can't be serious." The words escaped before she could stop them. "Dad," she took a breath, "mister feet-on-the-ground wrote this stuff? Believed another form of man walks the planet, pretending to be just like everyone else. Practicing magic?"

Katherine pulled to the edge of her chair, stood, handed Morey the manuscript. "You asked." She walked past Morey without giving her so much as a backward glance. "I'm going to get some coffee, start breakfast."

Stunned, Morey turned. Katherine was already out the library doors.

Morey stood, the manuscript dangling in her hand. She was unnerved by her reaction to the word magic. It was like a switch was thrown releasing a million megawatts of electricity. She plopped down into the chair, placed the manuscript on her lap. This was not the father she'd known. He'd have never stood for even a half-hearted conversation about such a ridiculous theory. She looked down at the manuscript and opened it.

21

Francis stared at the laptop screen, at his last entry in his journal - on the day he shut tight the door to deciphering the hieroglyphics.

The glyphs remain inscrutable. Though perhaps not in my life, I feel persuaded a key surer than the Rosetta stone will be discovered. I am at the end. I fear my mind is no longer clear. The glyphs do not match my original sketch. Something has changed.

That feeling Francis had the day he met Feuer, that Feuer had been in his office before, was right. Feuer or somebody had exhumed his journal, his research, and scanned them into the computer, all nice and neatly packaged and ready for the day they chose to thaw him out. They needed him to crack the glyphs and were using his daughter's life as a bargaining chip. What would happen to her if he couldn't pull this off?

An hour ago Protsky had removed the restraining straps, left Francis with the laptop. "You won't be going anywhere. We're cruising at forty thousand feet. Take your time. Unwrap my little present," Protsky nodded toward the laptop screen. "Read it all. Digest it thoroughly."

Francis looked around now. He was alone in a roomy area of four seats. A curtain divider in front was closed. He guessed this was a private jet. He looked down at the laptop at an icon marked Ground Zero. He clicked on it. He was surprised to find Protsky wanted him to see scanned copies of old newspaper clippings. He scrolled slowly through, reading each one, and then focused on the last.

<u>World's Largest Concentration of White Rhino Disappear</u>.
Hluhluwe-Umfolozi, South Africa

An undercover sting operation, hopeful of cracking a rhinoceros horn smuggling network, canceled its "Stop Poaching" operation. Endangered Species Protection Unit Police out on patrol reported seeing strange lights in the sky followed by the disappearance of all animals at a watering hole, including ten white rhino. ESPU police are currently searching the remainder of the wildlife park but continue to report all rhinos missing.

The divider curtain opened. Protsky stepped inside holding a glass of water. He walked to Francis and put the glass down next to the laptop.

"I suppose it's OK for you to have this now. Drink it slowly."

Francis drained the glass. With each swallow, the metallic taste lessened. "Where are we going with all this?" his voice was less hoarse; the water helped. He put the glass down, motioned to the laptop screen. "Every one of these newspaper articles reports the disappearance of wildlife. This last from South Africa mentions strange lights in the sky."

"Good, you picked that up," Protsky wiped a thin film of sweat from his top lip with his tongue. "Of course the NSA sent men, sent them after each event. They talked to local people and although sometimes a little persuasion was necessary, there was always at least one person willing to talk about what he'd seen. Here's the pattern at each and every one of these places," he closed a small, pudgy fist then extended a fat index finger, "first, strange anomalies in gravitational, electromagnetic fields," the second finger rose, "next strange lights in the sky, and last," he waved three fingers, "the disappearance of wildlife."

Francis stared at Protsky.

Protsky looked annoyed. "You're supposed to be the quintessential puzzle solver. Don't you get it?" When Francis did not answer, Protsky puffed out his chest haughtily. "My conclusion is that at these locations a door opened and closed. As bizarre as it sounds, someone, somehow, is creating a hole in the sky, and wildlife is being transported through," he hesitated, "a doorway."

Francis suddenly got the chills. The Buttu Highlands, a vision of the huge circular landscape filled with animal bones flashed through his mind. *As if they had all come here one day to wait.* At the center, human bones, one human, and the cylinder. Was this a failed attempt?

"So you're telling me the government believes aliens are stealing our wildlife. For what purpose?" Francis needed to keep things close to the vest. He needed to know how close they were to the community.

"I believe it's to save them." Protsky's voice was flat, emotionless. "A commonality of each place: the wildlife was either in immediate danger or was an endangered species. And no one said anything about aliens."

"Have you visited any of these places?" Francis asked.

"Just the last, and I spoke with one of the witnesses myself, a Bantu named Mbokwe who, after some prodding," Protsky smiled slyly, "claimed to have seen a miracle. Unfortunately for him, his family and friends think he's gone bonkers."

Francis didn't like Protsky, didn't like him a bit. "What exactly did he see?"

"He described beautiful lights in the sky, something similar to the Aurora Borealis. Here, listen." Protsky moved the mouse, clicked on the icon marked ESPU/Southern Africa.

Francis heard the voice of a man with an African accent. He sounded nervous, but when he started describing the lights in the sky, his voice changed dramatically. He sounded like a man possessed.

An arch of light stretched across the sky. So beautiful. Bands of colored light layered on top of each other pushing each layer closer and closer to the earth. Down, down it flowed, waving and swirling. The colors began to bleed together, drip into each other like running paint. The lights formed a giant, circular, glowing curtain. It was all around you, everywhere you turned, everywhere on the horizon. Everywhere! The curtain slowly waved as if God's breath were gently touching it. At the bottom of the curtain, waves rippled, touching the earth, curling and bending like a mirage. I wanted to touch it, run into it, let it consume me, disappear.

The recording ended. The African made it sound mesmerizing, powerful.

And it made sense. There would be colored lights, an aurora. Protsky had said the electromagnetic fields had changed. Something was creating a huge amount of energetic magnetic radiation. Like the geomagnetic storms from sunspots that travel to the Earth, enter our atmosphere, and cause the auroras at the Earth's poles.

"Did he say anything else?"

"Just before the light show started, he claims to have seen a huge black hole in the sky."

"Your doorway."

"Bull's-eye," Protsky sounded pleased.

"And you believe the cylinder and the phenomena are connected?"

"The people I work for think so. We just don't know how. That's where you come in."

"Have you seen this other cylinder?"

Protsky smiled, "Of course."

"And the owner?"

"An unfortunate accident, I'm told."

"I see." Francis's mouth went dry. He swallowed hard. His mind reeled. They were closing in on the community, had already killed to get their hands on a cylinder. If they needed Morey's, he had no doubt they'd do the same. He turned his head, looked toward the plane's curved window; saw Protsky's reflection, his face watching him. He had met other scientists like Protsky, individuals rushing to conclusions, manipulating data to get the results they wanted. Arrogant, patronizing, caught up in the pursuit of the golden ring, Protsky thought he'd trapped the very person who would help him win the grand prize and make him king.

Francis turned back, looked at Protsky.

Protsky's flat eyes gleamed. "I invite you to join me on this most incredible scientific expedition," his voice was full of hubris. "I think you'd agree it has no parallel. No one is closer to these hieroglyphics. If anyone can decode them, you can."

"I'm telling you they're undecipherable."

Protsky looked at him with a bemused smile. "Things have changed since you last tried."

"What are you talking about?"

"My computer, old boy. You didn't have the benefit of my correlation program," his voice oozed self-importance. "A program with my signature specifically designed to tackle our little puzzle, programmed into one and only one computer and I can sit you right in front of it."

"You think a computer can solve this?"

Protsky flushed. "All right then, I'll tell my people you don't want to play." He reached over, hit a few computer keys, the laptop screen went blank. "Sorry old man. Your daughter will be sorry too."

Protsky's arrogance finally triggered something deep within Francis, a well of outrage he tried to keep capped. Protsky read him and laughed dismissively.

"I want to meet your people," Francis said.

"Good, change of heart. Take a look out the window."

Francis leaned in, looked out the window. On the glimmering ocean below he could see whitecaps. The plane had descended.

"Northeast," Protsky said.

Francis craned his neck and recognized a feature like no other. "We're going to Apoquaque?"

"Uncanny, isn't it? Apoquaque has started to experience pre-phenomena anomalies, small almost undetectable shifts in the electromagnetic field – precursors, but no, look beyond Apoquaque."

Francis saw it then. A ship. An aircraft carrier.

"The US Falcon," Protsky confirmed. "A navy vessel loaded with computers and most importantly, my computer."

"Why not work directly on Apoquaque?" Francis wanted to get as close to Morey as possible.

"This is a clandestine operation. My understanding is Apoquaque islanders have their antennas out for strangers, much better to sit nice and tight on the Falcon."

Francis's mind spun. Morey was on Apoquaque, surrounded by the community. What was she learning? What would be her initiation? Did the community know how close the NSA was to learning about them? Would they be able to protect Morey or themselves?

"One more question. What the NSA's involvement in all of this?"

"The NSA," Protsky smirked. "They're drooling. They would do anything to get their hands on this technology. Think about what this would mean. Guaranteed superiority. When the next door opens, they want the Falcon there ready and waiting."

22

Morey opened her father's manuscript. She read what was printed at the center of the first page.

Magic, some believe, comes from evil. Others say it is a link to what is divine. Its source remains a mystery, with one thing undisputable - magic is inherited through blood.

She turned the page. Incredibly, the next page was printed in Eqyptian-like symbols. She turned to the next page, then the next. The entire thesis was in hieroglyphics - a language clearly different than her cylinder's glyphs but ancient nonetheless. Her father was proficient in the ancient languages and had chosen to write his thesis in one that only a master could translate. Why?

Her mother's gift lay lightly around her neck, the pendant faintly radiating a small circle of heat where it touched her chest. Her hand rose to it. Hill had said she knew her sea lion. How could she? She tried to put her thoughts in any order that would make sense. Last night's dinner was like a scene from some play where every character but she knew what was going on. The fable of the wolf-dogs, the cylinder opening, Ethel's foreboding toast on the porch - it all left her with a sense of agitated anticipation, like one waiting for the proverbial axe to fall, then today, the icing on the cake - her father's theory about Homo occultus and the strange indecipherable manuscript.

She thought of the emptiness she'd always felt after waking from her dream. She recognized now this hollowness had always been with her, this hole that she needed to fill. Now she felt with it an irresistible appetite to make some sense of the mystery surrounding the cylinder and her necklace as if her life depended on it. Yet deep within flowed a subtle current, a suggestion that it might be more than she'd wanted to know.

Morey replaced the manuscript among the other books on the bookshelves. She needed to talk with Aunt Katherine. She walked out of the library, through the central hall, and peered into the kitchen and dining room. Empty. She bounded up the staircase to the second floor, listened. No Katherine. She went up the spiral stairs to the tower room, dressed hurriedly, jeans, tee-shirt, sneakers, then returned downstairs to the porch.

She grasped the porch railing with both hands, leaned out toward the garden, still no Katherine.

"Rwoof."

She turned toward the soft bark. Across the road, sitting exactly where she had last seen them disappear, were the wolf-dogs from the pier.

"Rrrwoof," the voice sounded sharper.

Morey looked into their eyes, golden, intense. "You two look quite alive to me."

"RRRwoof."

"OK, OK. I'll come say hello."

Morey descended the porch steps and crossed the road to the meadow. As she came within fifteen feet of the dogs, they bolted and disappeared into the tall grasses. Morey knelt down on one knee and parted the reeds. She saw the dogs' furry rumps as they moved in fluid silence on a trail so perfectly shaped by them that nothing interrupted their speed. Everywhere was grass meadow, except for this Alice-in-Wonderland tunnel containing the flowing fantasy canines. She stood up and watched the grass ocean feather, keeping its visitors secret. The tunnel broke sky at a knoll where both dogs turned and barked for her to follow.

Morey looked back at the house and thought of going back, leaving a note. But what would she say? That she was off following two ghost dogs on their rounds?

"Rrwoof," the dog with the silver-gray coat was losing patience.

Morey parted the grasses and entered the camouflaged track. Her legs chilled as dew soaked through her jeans. She quieted her steps to imitate the dogs' silent paws, then tumbled into the raw, physical pleasure of the pace. She ran with them. The grass meadow gave way to brush. Birds swept into the lattice of bramble branches. Brush gave way to woods, ancient woods dense with undergrowth. Mosses and lichens in greens and grays lapped up the bases of trees, clothed gnarled tree roots. Running in the cool, high woods, she struggled to keep up. Sun fell through the treetops, straight beams in slightly misted air, and with each pass through she sensed a change like her camera shutter opened, closed, and opened again to a new reality. With each pass, a white-hot heat streamed through her legs, her legs felt stronger, the run easier, she swifter.

The dogs paused. She caught up to them. The silver looked directly into Morey's eyes. It was an intelligent look, a penetrating look. However brief, it telegraphed its message implicitly: For now, you are a member of our pack. Be one with us. Trust us. Follow us. We will direct you.

The run continued, and the run was all that mattered. A branch caught the bridge of her nose. It smarted. Her top lip felt warm, wet. She licked it. Blood, salty, delicious. A stream of primal energy shot through her, reshaped her, made her drunk with the suspension of muscle on bone.

The dogs stopped, sat down on their haunches. She joined them. They were at the bluffs, a part she had never been to before. She examined the beach cove below. Leading down was a steep narrow rock path that ended one hundred yards to the left. There, a craggy ocean-rock peninsula jutted out into the water. What was beyond was hidden from sight. Morey looked out to the water. The ocean stretched out glimmering in the sun. In the distance, Morey saw Little Apoquaque, a mere speck of rock and sand off Apoquaque Main.

The silver dog spoke a soft "Rrhorr," and nudged Morey's shoulder with his nose as if admonishing her to pay attention. With his face only inches from hers, the dog's intelligent, amber eyes conveyed pleasure, acknowledgment that Morey had done well as a member of his pack. Another soft bump with his nose, and her face was treated to a long circular sniff. Soft fur delicately tickled her skin. The silver backed away and stretched long, head down, rump up, front legs fully extended, toes spread wide. Then in unison, the dogs turned and headed back into the woods. After a few yards, they simultaneously began to wag their tails, and then they were gone.

Morey knew she was not meant to follow. She was where they intended her to be. She was on her own. She looked down at the immaculate deserted beach. Curling translucent water crashed with bassoon roars into white foam and spray. She noticed dark objects hitching a ride in the surf. Shiny black heads cut through a wave wall. Sea lions.

At least a dozen sea lions were it seemed to her, enjoying the best surfing on the island. Two rode in on a gigantic wave. One sea lion was sleek, agile in its shore landing, dancing and barking his enjoyment, his flippers splashing ocean spray. The other one landed heavily in the sand. She watched it push up out of the sand and was surprised. It was a woman in a black wet suit. She pulled off her headpiece. Hill.

Hill turned, faced the bluffs, and looked up in her direction. Morey felt all the misgivings of a peeping tom. She thought of darting behind a tree, but Hill saw her, extended her arm, and waved, inviting her down. The sea lion plunged back into the sea. She watched the sea lions' heads bobbing in the surf, as one by one they disappeared into deeper water. Then Morey started down the narrow path leading to the beach where Hill waited.

Katherine opened the kitchen window and looked out to a patch of green grass next to her garden. There was no wind outside, a perfect day to be out on the water. She held up her hands. Her fingers were long, still strong but thinner, the flesh translucent. She remembered the little girl who played on the grass by her garden.

She remembered Francis, a young father bending down to his little girl, letting her whisper little-girl secrets in his ear. She watched him stiffen, straighten up. Katherine understood. Francis was terrified, terrified as much for his daughter as of her. He thought if he hid the truth from her, the truth would change. But Katherine knew the truth would someday call to Morey. Half of Morey starved for it.

She looked at them standing hand and hand on her patch of grass, watched Francis let the little girl's hand go. She saw the hurt on the little girl's face, then the familiar blurring of colors, the softening around the edges of things, the running together. She put her fingers to her eyes and wiped away the tears forming there, and when she did, everything became clear again.

23

"**S**o this is how you send for me?" Morey narrowed her eyes, gave Hill her this-should-be-interesting look.

Hill smiled a ragged, apologetic smile. She stared at Morey's nose with the concerned look of a parent whose child had gotten into it with the neighborhood bully. Morey saw a brief flicker of pride. Then Hill turned, entered the water and knee-deep, pushed to a rubberized raft floating in a pool of water sheltered by the dark, basaltic rocks of the jetty.

"A hello would be nice," Morey muttered to herself. She felt the bridge of her nose. There was a small lump there and the ragged skin of a thin scratch. She looked down at her disheveled, dirt encrusted tee-shirt smeared with pinesap and pulled it straight. She was sure she'd perfectly captured the look of a professional hog wrestler.

She watched Hill clear the raft of the rocks, push it toward shore, and motion for her to sit at the bow. She was all business.

Morey pulled off her sneakers and socks, left them on the beach, rolled up her jeans, and waded into the cold water. Hill steadied the raft as Morey swung in, and then she waited as Morey maneuvered to the bow and sat facing out to sea. Morey felt the bob of Hill swinging in, then the engine started, lurched into gear, and they flew over the surf past the natural jetty and out to open water.

Suddenly, Hill swung the raft hard into a u-turn back to shore. Morey tried to balance herself, almost tumbling over. Straight ahead she saw the small mouth of a cave. She looked up at the bluffs and determined anyone looking down would see nothing but a sheer drop to water. It was only from exactly where they were, out on the water and dead straight on at that, that the narrow opening became visible. Hill sped the raft straight for the image of a half-opened mouth, its stone lips twisted, almost curled.

"Duck," Hill yelled.

Morey flattened herself. The raft barely threaded into a tiny tunnel. She felt the top of her head brush the slick ceiling, cold droplets trickling down the back of her neck. Instantly, the temperature dropped as if someone just opened a freezer door.

Hill cut the engine, and the raft glided out of the tunnel's mouth onto the glassy water of a voluminous cave. Quiet enveloped them. The raft sailed on a black liquid mirror past gas lanterns hung from spikes driven into rock walls. The lanterns lit the water in soft circles, reflections played on wet ebon walls. Morey watched their shadows, monstrous and distorted stalk them as they floated forward toward platforms anchored on floating oil drums. She looked further into the cave, and saw how the black got denser, took in substance, filled in every space. This was a place of in-betweens. In between light and dark, between above ground and below ground, the limbo land. The cave was a chamber of shape-shifting, of image disengaging, reforming, and harboring a mystery.

"Welcome to my office," Hill said matter-of-factly, "and current home."

"You live here, inside a cave?" She thought of caves as barren places, their insides emptied out, their rooms vacant. Not at all the kind of place you'd call home.

Hill laughed. It was the first time Morey had heard her laugh. She liked it. It was smooth, generous, calming.

Hill threw a rope over a wooden mooring and secured the raft. "Most of my work is conducted at sea." She grabbed the mooring, swung up easily onto the platform. Hill looked down at Morey for a moment and extended her hand to her. "Let me show you around."

She rested one hand on the mooring for balance, placed the other into Hill's. She felt herself lifted up, and then there she was, standing inches from Hill so close she could not bring herself to look into her face. She looked down at the platform floor, waited a long moment for

Hill to turn and walk on. When she did, Morey wished the moment back.

"As you can see, this whole construction is meant to float up and down with the tide." Hill bounced up and down on the platform, and the platform dipped and rose under their feet. "Cables driven into the cave walls secure it from the pull of the outgoing tide. Charlie claims this is an old pirate cave. High tide closes the cave's mouth, but the natural ledges stay nice and dry above water level, perfect for stashing bounty." Hill looked back at Morey, and her gaze caught hers briefly. "At high tide, the only way to get in or out is to hold your breath, dive, and swim through."

"Kind of spooky," A shiver of claustrophobia shot through Morey.

"Over here is all my equipment." Hill moved forward, stopped in front of a row of three computers. Their electronic light washed up the curving cave wall.

Morey moved to the computers. She let her eyes wander to the unintelligible stream of data washing across the screens. The screens winked and blinked lines of ever-changing letters and numbers. She thought how long Hill must have worked to construct this 'office', concluded she had not done so alone.

There was a light wind, a coolness wafted out from somewhere, a wind that smelled distinctively old. Looking down at the screen of every changing data, her hair, light and curly in the humidity, lifted away from her face. It felt as if Hill had circled back behind her and breathed down her neck, sending a breeze forward over her ears, surrounding her face.

She swung around and faced Hill accusingly.

Hill looked amused. "This is a breathing cave," she said.

Morey watched wisps of Hill's hair lift off her neck too, then in a couple of seconds Hill's hair changed direction, lifted away from her forehead.

"Changes in barometric pressure of wind turbulence outside the cave's mouth cause the air to move in through the small tunnel and out the mouth, then it reverses. Sometimes you barely notice it."

"Oh," Morey said weakly and admonished herself to stay focused. "Awfully fancy equipment." She got back on subject.

"Extremely fancy stuff," Hill agreed. She seemed unconcerned, detached from the obviously strange impression a cave laboratory would make.

"So all this stuff you set up in this cave to protect it from - from the weather?"

Hill ignored her question, motioned her to a screen. "This computer acts as a seismograph and contour map. Here," she pointed. "This is the contour of the ocean floor right in front of our cave." Hill punched the keypad. Her face darkened. "Here's the ocean floor surrounding the oil rig. The red dot is the rig." Her finger brushed the screen. "This line signifies the fault Herman Bristol is concerned about."

"I can see why." Morey bent over the screen. "They're on top of one another." She looked at Hill. A thin line of dried sea salt crusted her right cheekbone. She smelled like the beach.

Hill stared down at that computer for a long moment. She looked as if her thoughts had gone somewhere else, somewhere foreboding. She startled Morey when she continued. "This computer collects and stores enormous amounts of information," she motioned to the second, softly humming machine. "Salinity of the water, ocean currents, temperature by depth, rock formation, and mineral make-up."

"And last," Hill turned to the third computer.

Morey looked over at endless rows of As, Ts, Gs, and Cs.

"The sequence of letters, short for adenine, thymine, quamine, and cytosine, represent the chemical groups of DNA. The computer is capable of laser-scanning blood samples and giving a personal genetic card or genome." Hill looked at her. "Right now you are looking at a genomic readout on a sea lion I call Tenor."

Morey's hand reached for and found the necklace's pendant, warm, somehow comforting.

"Is Tenor my sea lion?" She felt uncomfortable asking questions. Why?

Hill punched in a code. The screen displayed a large wheel composed of shaded bands. "Here," Hill continued. "You can check on how each sea lions is doing."

Because Hill wasn't answering them.

"Extraordinary. So you are studying these sea lions because?" Morey raised her shoulders, extended her arms, a gesture of her confusion.

"The why is a little more difficult," there was reluctance in Hill's voice. She took in a deep breath, was quiet again.

Morey thought Hill was considering how to reply. Then Hill looked at her in a tender way that made Morey feel as if she wanted to protect her. Strangely, a flash of anger crossed Hill's face and was gone.

It was unsettling. Then she got it. Was struck by it. She had no idea where this revelation came from, but it was acute. Hill looked at her and saw death. The death of someone close, someone she'd loved deeply. In Hill's face she read the understanding that no one was safe from it. No one had any protection from it. Morey felt her heart thudding.

"Why all this?" Morey was surprised by the force in her tone.

"The why, Morey, has to do with your cylinder, your quest."

A vision of Ethel raising her glass, toasting to Morey's heritage flashed through her mind. She took a step back from Hill and held fast to the little stone sea lion around her neck. Holding the pendant somehow helped. "What are you saying?"

Hill's faced darkened. Her body stiffened. "We need to start." Her look was intense. It frightened Morey. "I want to take you to your sea lion now."

Suddenly Morey was in no hurry. She started to move away from Hill, stopped when Hill lifted her hand.

"Isn't this what you wanted?" Hill said.

"What do you mean?"

"A solution to your mystery."

"What are you talking about?"

"Don't you want to know why you have this cylinder?"

"Of course I do. So you're saying you know?" Morey's voice echoed off the cave walls. "But this is—"

"We will start with a promise." Hill cut her off.

A promise. Whose promise? She did not want to be making promises.

"Your promise," Hill said, as if she had read Morey's mind. "You must promise to keep an open mind and be patient - patient in waiting for things to unfold. I call the shots." Hill looked hard at Morey, her eyes narrowing.

"Look. You said you knew my sea lion, nice and simple. Now things are getting a little crazy."

"Crazy? This is just the start. Are you in or out?"

"Of what exactly?"

"Your quest. The thing you must learn. I can teach you."

"You?"

"If you pass the test, you go on."

"What test?"

"That will come later."

"And who determines if I pass?"

"I do. Your opinion doesn't matter."

Morey stiffened. Suddenly things were happening much too quickly. She stopped, folded her arms across her chest. "You expect me to go into this - this crazy quest thing - blind, just obeying *your* orders?" She glared at Hill.

"Correct."

"You realize this is insane."

Hill stared back at her. "Time is short."

"Why should I trust you?"

"Trust me or don't trust me," Hill shrugged, "but trust your instincts."

Instincts. Her instincts told her she did not like being the one in the dark while Hill held all the cards. Hill said she knew why Morey had the cylinder. Hill said she could teach her. Teach her what? Hill would be in control. She hated it. She'd risked life and limb before but always on her own terms. Her thoughts spun in small tight circles. She needed a solution to her mystery, Hill was right. But it was take it or leave it, Hill's way or no way. She was alone in a cave laboratory with the Phantomess of Cave Lake who was basically telling her to give up her control.

"We will start with a promise," she heard Hill repeat, "to be open and patient."

No one else had offered any other solutions. It was this or nothing. "Well?"

"OK." She screwed up her face, letting Hill know she was not happy with this contract. She thought I can do this open and patient thing, can't I?

"OK what?" Hill was pushing it.

"OK, I promise."

"Promise what?"

"I promise to be open and patient." She wanted to add yes, master, I'll do anything you want, master, but thought better of it.

Surprisingly, Hill looked at her with admiration. "You'll need a wet suit. The waters are chilly. You'll find one in the back that fits you," she gestured to an area past the computers, to the last platform buttressed against a curving cave wall. "I'll wait at the raft." Hill turned and left.

"This is insane," Morey murmured. She spun around and looked to the back of the cave to the last platform. She felt wired, like an animal must when the trapdoor shuts with a bang, and it realizes there's no way out. She followed the walkway, past a dangling showerhead and hose that disappeared into black cave water, to a sleeping cot. Laid out on the cot were a wet suit, a camera, and a card.

She picked up the camera and turned in over in her hands. It was a bright yellow Reefmaster CL underwater camera. She put it back down and reached for the card.

Dear Morey,

    Nothing would make me happier than a spread of your photography in the Apoquaque Free Press!

    Love, Ethel

She looked back at Hill now at the raft, her back politely to her. She tossed the card on the cot.

"Fine," she said.

She peeled off her clothing.

The wet suit fit perfectly.

24

Feuer hunched in the semi-vee concealed behind the jetty's walls. When Morey and Hill's raft came out of the cave, he waited till the raft was a mere dot on the ocean's surface. Then he steered the boat toward the mouth of the cave. The aluminum hull scraped the slick wet walls. As the tunnel constricted, he flattened himself onto the boat's floor, his head barely above the top of the engine, just high enough to steer. He thought the boat was going to get jammed, but suddenly it popped out of the mouth like a cork and glided into the huge cave.

He'd seen many clandestine operations, but this place was cut from a James Bond movie. He turned up the throttle, sped to the pier. He tied the boat up to the mooring, hoisted himself up, and looked at his watch. If Hill and Morey got back before he was done, he'd have to kill them. Graham would not be happy with that. As pleased as Graham was that Feuer obtained Anchor's cylinder, he was angry she had died, which made Feuer feel he had failed. He knew Graham thought nothing of eliminating people, but Graham had been clear. For now, he needed Morey to stay the cylinder's walking, talking owner. So today's job was to get in and get out with as much information as possible, with no one the wiser and no one dead.

He walked to the computers. One was clearly a contour map. He pulled a pencil-thin camera from his shirt pocket, focused on the screen and snapped. He moved to the other, ran his hand around its body looking for the drive. It had none. No way to download. He saw a large wheel composed of shaded bands on the screen. He scrolled down, flew through maybe twenty pages. He recognized it all as something having to do with DNA. He went back, started from the beginning, and snapped a picture of each screen. Then his attention was drawn to something shiny behind him. It was the boat. It seemed much higher in the water than when he had left it. In fact, he felt higher. The floating dock seemed higher. His gaze flew to the cave's mouth - almost gone.

Stupid. He hadn't thought to check the tide tables. He had to get out of there. Fast.

He ran to the boat, untied it, jumped in, and started the engine. He sped to the cave wall. Somewhere now submerged was the cave's mouth, his only way out. He cut the engine, grabbed at a slick rock jutting from the cave wall. He pulled the boat as close to the wall as he could, leaving space for his arm, steadied it, then pushed his arm into the black water. Not here. He grasped at another rock, tried to move the boat along the wall but his hand slipped, bashing his knuckles, cutting them open.

He took his gun from its shoulder harness, stood up, and waited for the boat to steady. He fired three shots into its floor, watched black water pool in. When the icy cold water reached his knees, he dove, swam to the cave wall. He moved slowly along the wall until he felt it - slightly warmer water flowing into the cave. He turned, waited impatiently till the boat slipped under, pumped air in and out of his lungs, held a lung-filling breath, and dove.

25

Morey sat at the bow, her back to Hill. She had neatly stacked her clothes, placed the camera on top, then deposited them on the raft floor beside her. She did not want to go back into the cave to retrieve them. The raft sped through open waters. Several gulls joined them, rushing low across the glittering water, easily keeping to the raft's speed. Morey breathed slowly, releasing air through her lips in gentle explosions. If she knew nothing else, she knew she would have to stay calm and alert and ready for anything.

Her thoughts spun in slow circles, spiraled in on her father. The man she remembered so full of restraint, self-control, distance. He chose a solitary profession, a career uncovering ancient mysteries, picking through fragments of things broken and drained of life's blood, a world dried and hardened. Stone by stone, he built a wall between himself and the human race. In her darker moments, she wondered whether she might have the same worm in her soul.

Question after question repeated in her mind. Why had her father waited so long to send her mother's gift? *The greatest theft of all is to rob one of the right to be.* Was her father admitting he'd robbed her of her right to be and if so, to be what exactly? Would her quest whatever it was, answer that question? And who was this woman, Hill? Why did she know so much about her quest?

"You'll need to know something about sea lions." She heard Hill's voice behind her. She swung herself around to face her and again was struck with how strongly she was attracted to her. She studied this woman whom she was expected to have blind faith in, to trust she could teach Morey about her quest. Hill looked at her, and this time

Morey held her gaze, searched in Hill's eyes, tried to read her. She saw fatigue, vulnerability, the look of a woman in trouble. She turned away. It was not what she wanted to see right now.

"I'll give you the Cliff Notes version." Hill's voice sounded clear and firm. She felt better.

"They belong to a family of marine mammals named Otariidea. One of the easiest ways of distinguishing sea lions from seals is their small, furry earflaps. Seawater is eight times denser than air, so their sleek, streamlined bodies move them through water without great energy. They swim four times faster than us, plunge to great depths, and shoot back like rockets. When they dive, their pupils dilate making their large eyes extremely light sensitive. The cornea has the same refractive index as water. A layer of silvery crystals behind the retina amplifies all light, making their sight superb. Where we would see very little or nothing, they see well enough to hunt. In the water, we lack directional hearing. Sounds seem to come from everywhere. The sea lion hears every sound with perfect distinctness. Their whiskers are supremely sensitive. They aid in navigation and the hunt for food." Hill cut the engine, let the raft drift. "There they are," Hill announced.

About three hundred yards to the right of their craft, sea lions leap out of the water and within seconds they were closer. Up popped sea lion heads. She counted five.

"Heads up," Hill yelled.

Morey had barely turned back to Hill when a snorkeling mask came flying toward her. She caught it just before it hit the raft's floor.

"In you go," Hill stated.

"Whoa, not so fast, Jacqueline Costeau."

"What's the matter? You can swim, can't you?"

"Of course I can swim," Morey shot back. "I just wasn't expecting - actually, I don't know what I was expecting. I mean really, how could I possibly know what to expect—" *Stop blathering*, she chastised herself.

"Your sea lion is waiting," Hill's tone was firm.

Morey looked at each of the five heads bobbing in their own undulating, concentric circles of water. Which one? If she didn't get in the

water, she'd never find out. *Go on, God damn it, just do it.* She had come
this far with two ghost dogs and a stranger who lived in a cave. What
was she afraid of now?

"Wake me up when you decide." Hill leaned back against the raft.

Morey shot Hill a look. She touched her pendant, moved it
between her index finger and thumb, and then zipped up the wet suit
over it. She picked up the mask, fit it tight to her face, and held it firm
with her left hand. With her right, she grabbed the camera and fell
in backward off the raft. She came up to clear her air hose and felt a
strong whoosh of water between her legs. She put her face underwater
and saw them.

Dark spindle shapes gliding effortlessly, full of curiosity. A sleek
shape swirled around her torso then was gone.

She started shooting. One dove, and she snapped it in a slow back
float beneath her, watching her with big round soft eyes. Another spun
tight circles around her as she followed, camera clicking. Then it surfaced with a rush and looped backward into the sea.

It seemed they performed a series of nautical aerobatics for her
camera, stayed with her until she stopped shooting. Then suddenly,
unexpectedly, with yet another whoosh of speed, all five swam out of
visual range.

She surfaced, pulled off her mask, and turned to face Hill. She felt
elated. "Wow! They're simply beautiful!" She swam to the raft, held out
her hand for a pull in.

Hill shook her head. "Not yet."

A sea lion's head broke water just three feet from Morey. It surprised her, and she splashed back. It was the smallest of the group.
Close up, the animal's puffed cheeks were like a lion's shot through
with long, thick, straw-like whiskers. Face-to-face, she saw the milky
white corneas of the creature's eyes. She was blind. Suddenly the joy of
Morey's experience was wrenched from her. The animal moved closer
and opening its huge nostrils nosily snorted her.

"She's memorizing your scent." Morey heard Hill from the raft.

Morey raised the camera and clicked. Then the sea lion touched
her with its nose, poked her gently in the belly. It felt wonderful. With

a splash, she was gone beneath the sea. Morey remembered her pendant—whiskers, ears, no eyes.

"Here, give me your hand," Hill called to her.

She swam to the raft, extended her hand and Hill pulled her in.

"She's OK, Morey." Hill had apparently sensed her sadness. "Blind sea lions can and do survive nicely because of all the other wonderful abilities I told you about. And your sea lion has developed them far better than any of her companions. She's very healthy. In fact, she's the leader of this group." Hill's gray-green eyes held hers. "Her name is Maker."

"Maker," Morey repeated the name, turning it over in her mind. "Will I meet Maker again?" For some reason, she could not bear the thought this would be their only meeting.

"Is that your wish?"

"Yes, very much. I feel silly saying this, but I feel a bond with her." Her hand moved to her stomach to where Maker had poked her. She let her gaze drop back to the water beneath the raft, searching for some sign of her.

"I understand completely. I care deeply about them, know them each as unique individuals. I would do anything to protect them."

Morey looked at Hill. The resolve of Hill's last statement was accentuated by a tightening of her face, a narrowing of her eyes, as if she already knew the day would come when she would have to take action.

Morey sat in silence, watched Hill start the engine. Then Morey swung around to face forward, her back to Hill as she guided the raft back to Apoquaque. Morey let the sun warm her face, the wind move through her hair, the experience with the sea lions soak in. Her life was changing. She was changing. She was traveling toward a new world and in order to get there, she must lose sight of the old. Hard firm ground had surely slipped away, and she needed to know where she was heading.

"Do I not deserve to know what is happening?" She attempted to sound clear, strong. She did not turn around to Hill. She knew she had promised patience, to let things unfold. When Hill did not respond, did not remind her of her promise, she continued. "My father protected me all my life from who I am, kept me away from Apoquaque, from knowledge of my mother."

"Perhaps your father was right to protect you."

She felt her pulse quicken. "If you truly believe that, why did you bring me out here to meet Maker?"

"There are some things I cannot change. You have a right to be here, to know who you are."

The anger rose in her like a firecracker. Patience was just not her forte - especially when someone knew something about her life that she herself did not know.

"You say I have a right to know who I am. So you think you know something I don't?' She swung around to face Hill. "Tell me then - who am I?"

Hill's gaze locked with hers. "You, Morey, are like me." Hill's face was so serious, almost pained. "Although your father's blood tainted your genetics, you are still your mother's daughter born of the same blood as our people, as me."

Blood. The word stuck out like a thorn. She remembered the words of the manuscript. *Magic is inherited through blood.*

"Your father threatened to expose our existence."

"What are you saying?"

"I think you know."

"You're telling me that Homo occultus stuff is true - that my mother was one of them. You are one of them! I'm—" She felt her heart beating, her pulse thudding in her ears. She started to get up, realized she had nowhere to go, sat back down.

"Then you know, you understand," Hill said.

"If I ever do, I absolutely insist you have me committed."

"Think Morey. Think."

She has the magic. The phone woman's voice played in Morey's mind.

"Think about the things that have happened to you. You cannot run from yourself," Hill continued.

Morey could not think. Her mind felt numb. Hill was right. What she wanted to do right now was run but something in her knew Hill was telling the truth - her disconnection from other people, her father's fear for her, of her. A tear escaped, ran down her cheek. "I believe I'm afraid of it." Morey confessed.

"Half of you is terrified. Your father's half. But the other half, the half that is of your mother, is thirsting for expression."

Some hoodoo was at work in her brain, which scared her when she dared to think about it. She valued her mind. It was her link with her independence, which was her mainstay, her anchor without which she'd be lost, afloat in a vast, indifferent sea with never the slightest hope of sighting land. But now something whispered in her mind, whispered of change, and she could not know what would be left of her, or even who she might be when the whispering ceased.

"Magic," Morey said softly.

"Magic that comes with responsibilities." Hill's voice was grave. "Magic that changes you. You are different from other people. A difference that marks you, a difference you must hide."

Morey suddenly felt sad for Hill, then frightened for herself. Her heart pounded louder. This woman she knew nothing about, with whom she was totally alone at the ocean's edge, knew things, things about her mother, about her, about magic.

She was at the door. She could choose to walk through it or stay where she was on the other side. The part of her that belonged to her father was screaming, setting off alarms. Loud blaring sirens.

She studied Hill's face, kissed by the sunlight. How could she possibly be frightened of her, frightened of anything she would share with her? Was this what she felt for Hill, the attraction of two animals of the same species, molded from the same DNA? Until now, they inhabited different worlds, yet they were the same - of the same blood.

"I have felt different all my life," Morey said wearily.

Hill said nothing.

"In my dream, my father spoke of the powers I have."

"You, as all of us, have the power to jump. But you must be taught how. This is what I can teach you." There was no pleasure in Hill's voice, as if this was an assignment she did not relish.

The shore was coming up fast; Morey felt the raft's bottom slide in and out of shallow water.

"Tomorrow morning, same place, same time, this time with scuba gear." Hill beached the raft and waited for her to get out.

Morey didn't want to leave. She felt dizzy with unanswered questions.

"And the jump?" She gave it a shot.

"All in good time," Hill shot her a look as if reminding her of her promise.

Morey grabbed her clothes, swung herself over the raft's side, stood knee deep in the chilly water. She watched the raft head out into open water away from the cave toward town. She shook herself as if the motion would clear her mind.

"This is totally crazy."

"Rwwhorrhhrr."

She turned toward the familiar salutation, looked up to the top of the bluffs.

26

Hill sped the raft to town. They would want a report, to know Morey's progress.

She stared at the bow where Morey had been sitting moments ago. The yellow Reefmaster camera sat on top of her snorkeling mask. Hill couldn't help liking her, the way she could reach inside herself to summon determination, courage. The open way she embraced Maker. Her ability to stay afloat with the changes, the inexplicable new forces and realities she faced. The way her face screwed up when she tried to hide her annoyance. Hill found her alluring.

Morey was tough too. Intelligent, capable of thinking on her feet, and she was supremely talented. The abilities she'd inherited from her mother ran strong in her blood. But despite her intelligence and abilities, she hadn't been born into this life like Hill had, like the rest of them. She hadn't been guided from birth, her talents nurtured and fine-tuned from day one. She would be taking all this on now. She would be expected to learn everything in a short period of time with Hill as her teacher, the teacher who had failed so miserably with Anchor.

Hill had refused the assignment, remained adamant. But then the elder came to her, came to her in her dreams.

"I cannot be the one to teach Morey," Hill told the elder.

"It must be you."

"I cannot," Hill insisted.

"She will want to please you."

"And that may kill her. She is only half us. She must choose our blood over her father's of her own determination. Not to please me. Or she will not survive."

Hill had awakened terrified.

Now what terrified Hill most was she was beginning to feel alive again. She'd felt this energy in the library, on the porch that night, over and over again in the cave, and on the raft today. She had tried to dismiss it, but she could not. It had taken on a life of its own. She was falling for Morey. And now she was as frightened for Morey's life as she was for her own without her.

It was dusk when Morey arrived at the Victorian. The house was empty, no sign of Katherine. She was glad to be alone. Her mind was swimming in a viscous liquid, like she'd been drugged. She knew this was exhaustion. She went into the kitchen, opened the refrigerator, took out some leftover Cornish hen, and poured herself a glass of milk. She was ravenous.

When she was finished eating, she left the kitchen and headed to the tower room. Night had come quickly. Cold, silent stars sparkled outside her tower room window. She stripped off her clothing and snuggled beneath the comforter, feeling her own weight pulling her down. She thought of her mother, remembered a childhood fantasy she played over and over when she was a child, her mother gazing down upon her in her crib. She lying there, looking up, and hearing a soft whooshing whirl. The soft whooshing whirl of three small spheres revolving around a larger glowing orb, all suspended in the air. Lying there, seeing and hearing, and feeling that this was miraculous.

When sleep came, Morey dreamed of music. The harmony of the spheres drifted and swelled and drifted again. Its current transmuted into an unearthly, haunting melodious song. Wild, beautiful, eerie howlings. A wolf-dog concert whose current resonated in her essence, her soul. Full-throated, great-hearted voices. Voices rich, each a different pitch, chording, never in unison, vaulting through the octaves, then trailing into light, ethereal notes. Entwining, spiraling around each other, reaching skyward toward the heavens. Sometimes there was a long, pure note of a solo, then a soulful voice would wrap around it. The song was pervasive, reverberating. The melody rose up and up into the infinite blackness of space, and once again, she heard the whirling music of the three spheres and felt her mother's radiance.

Her mother spoke to her.

Remember this moment. It is your anchor. It will provide for you.

27

Rupert Cirrus stood outside the high, tapering doors of the quaint brick building and rang the bell. The building was one of many scattered around the world, owned by the community for centuries. Small brass numbers were screwed into the door, but he knew no one but the community visited here. No mail was ever delivered. No FedEx packages celebrating birthdays, anniversaries arrived. He heard the mechanical hum of the lock, the pop of the deadbolt. He opened the door and stepped inside.

He waited for his eyes to adjust to the dim light. Floor-to-ceiling murals painted the walls of a long corridor - African plains, South American rainforest, tundra scenes. It seemed his eyes had drifted over these scenes a thousand times. He walked the corridor and stopped in front of a mural depicting the tree of life. Hidden within its bark, clinging to its limbs, lying by its massive trunk were the images of all the animals of the Earth. Above the tree were words from *The Outermost House* by Henry Beston:

> *For the animal shall not be measured by man. In a world older and more complete than ours, they move finished and complete, gifted with extensions of the senses we have lost or never attained, living by voices we shall never hear. They are not brethren, they are not underlings; they are other nations, caught with ourselves in the net of life and time, fellow prisoners of the splendor and travail of the earth.*

He continued down the corridor and entered the antechamber.

The room was large with a high ceiling, lit by candle wall sconces and candle chandeliers. A massive fireplace ten men could step into was the room's heat source. There was no electricity, no phones, no bills to be traced. The community was made up of men and women from different walks of life: stockbrokers, lawyers, doctors, businessmen. They poured their wealth back into the community to support the cultural imperative. And of course there were the warriors - the ones who jumped.

Several children sat quietly on oriental rugs, books strewn at their feet. Lessons. A young woman with shiny black hair clasped at the back of her neck in a silver dragonfly brooch sat on the rug with them. She looked up at him as he entered. Her almond-shaped eyes were soft and kind.

"Xiaoning," he winked at her.

The woman smiled, nodded.

She spoke softly to the young boy sitting cross-legged by her side. The boy looked up at Rupert, eyes filled with awe. She spoke again to the boy and gave him a gentle nudge. He rose, ran toward the fireplace and wiggled in between two chairs facing the hearth. The boy laid some kindling into the huge grate, then put a few sticks and a large log on top of it. Then he struck a long match and lighted the fire. In a second, the kindling was popping and snapping. The boy stared down into the flames. Then smiling, he ran back to her side and sat down.

Long ago, Rupert had taken lessons in this very room. Running on spindly legs to bookcases covered by glass doors at play with reflected firelight, he'd pull out a book and run back to the thick Oriental rug to his teacher. The hieroglyphic print came easy to him. He consumed the ancient knowledge.

The fire was blazing strongly now, the delicious aroma comforting, the thick log engulfed in bright orange flames. The warmth of the fire had spread throughout the room. It surrounded him and held him like a blanket. In the back of the room, a group of men and women his age sat in a circle on worn leather chairs, reading orders, making plans. Rupert saw the elder's hand resting on a chair's arm - fingers thinned by age, fragile, blue veins standing out. His teacher.

He walked to the fireplace, slowly sat down on the warm floor beside the hearth, and leaned against the stone, letting its heat warm his back. The fire gave off its low crackling, and the flames danced against the floorboards. The motion seemed entirely too slow to be real. Rupert looked up into the elder's face. Her thin fingers dug into the upholstery as she inched forward in the chair, her expression intent. He heard her silent mental command in his mind.

"Anchor's cylinder. You must destroy it."

"And what of Francis Chance?"

"He will determine his own fate."

28

Francis found the US Falcon extraordinary. If nothing else, its enormity exceeded what his civilian mind had anticipated. He literally got a bird's-eye view as he gaped through the plane's window.

When they landed, Protsky and he were whisked off to separate quarters. The sense he got from the little he was able to observe en route, sandwiched between two mute naval escorts, was that the ship was on high alert. The ensign stationed outside his cabin door announced there was to be a meeting at 0900 and shut his door. It was a sparely furnished room. Neatly folded on a small cot was a military-style jumpsuit with a multitude of zippered pockets. On top of that was a pair of black, polished military boots. Two red lights covered by black wire baskets stood out in the room. One hung on the wall above the door, directly over a clock, the other above the bathroom mirror. Alarm lights? He looked at the clock. He had twenty minutes to shower and change.

He stripped off his clothes. He'd noticed from the walk on deck and the several flights of stairs he'd negotiated to get to his room that his body felt weak. He guessed this was a consequence of being 'on ice', as Protsky had described it. He also noticed how sharp his mind was, sharper than it had been in years, maybe ever. Yet something disturbed him. He could not quite put his finger on it, but there was a sense of foreignness, like something was in his brain that had never been there before. He kept trying to focus on it. What was it exactly? But it remained just out of reach. He didn't like it.

The warm watery needles of the shower stung his flesh, helped his muscles come alive. The soap washed away the soiled sense permeating his being. Protsky's closeness on the plane had assaulted his sensibilities. His mere presence was an affront. When he stepped out of the shower and dried himself off, he felt cleansed, human again. He zipped up the front of his military garb, looked at himself in the mirror. He pushed his shoulders back, stood straight. He certainly looked the part. Then he leaned in, looked dead on at his face. The man gazing back looked much older than Francis remembered, sadder, a little desperate. He stared deeper into his own reflected eyes, looked for a glimpse of that foreignness. Transfixed by his own dark pupils he was drawn into a labyrinth branching, descending, constricting, what was around the corner just out of sight. It was as if he was trying to access another dimension, access some hidden room from which a force whirls out and spins in and sits down entirely still and looks back at you. It scared him.

Two sharp knocks on ship's metal startled him. Francis opened his door.

"Follow me, sir," the sailor said.

Francis stepped out, closing the door behind him. He followed the sailor down a corridor and up two flights of stairs. Along the way, he noticed more red lights protected by black wire-mesh baskets. Finally, they entered a large circular room with electronic equipment packed against its curved walls. In front of each monitor was a sailor focused on the changing data on his computer screen. Standing in the middle of the room was Protsky.

"Welcome to heaven!" Protsky beamed, theatrically extending his arms in a grand sweep of the room.

The room reminded Francis of something out of science fiction, maybe the flight deck from a Star Trek movie. There was another door directly opposite the one through which he had entered. White fluorescent light outlined its edges. Some ten feet from the door the metal wall became a glass wall and in the middle of it was a glass door. He could tell there was a small room behind, but from where he stood he could not see into it.

"Impressed?" Protsky puffed out his chest, did not wait for his response. "This is our command center. I'll give you the real cook's tour later. We're about to be briefed." Protsky walked to the door outlined in fluorescent light, pushed it open, waited for him to follow.

They entered a shoebox-narrow room containing a long, rectangular conference table. Francis was surprised by what he saw. Sitting ramrod straight in crisp uniforms were four officers. He knew by the insignia that one of them was the captain, odd that the captain sat with his men. At the head of the table was the strangest looking man he had ever seen - snow-white hair, linen-white skin, dark sunglasses. The meeting was already in progress.

"Welcome, Dr. Chance." The strange man smiled at him. "Please be seated. I'll make the introductions."

Francis looked at Protsky. Protsky motioned for him to take a seat. He sat down in the chair in front of him, farthest from the man. Protsky sat next to him.

"Please excuse the sunglasses - a genetic eye condition." The pale man leaned forward. "First let me introduce Captain Harrow and his men." His tone was derisive. One long, elegant white hand, then another came out from under the table. The right motioned gracefully toward the captain.

The captain was young with a nearly skin-close Afro. He exuded a strict, military stiffness. "Dr. Chance," he said through clenched teeth. The other officers remained silent.

The linen-white man's head moved back to Francis, dark lenses impenetrable. "Gabriel Graham at your service. I hope you'll be at mine." He smiled at Francis the way men smile when they like what they see.

Francis did not know how to take him. There was something androgynous about him, snake-like about him, his shiny opaque black lens moving as his alabaster face moved with King cobra grace. He wondered if he really had an eye condition or if the glasses offered some sick psychological edge he enjoyed.

"Captain Harrow has temporarily given command of the US Falcon to me." Graham said, his long hands rubbing together like a fly's legs. He turned to the captain. "Continue."

Francis watched the muscles in Harrow's face contorting; the officer next to the captain sweating. The captain gave the man a quick nod at which the junior officer rose, walked over to a map hanging on the wall, and picked up a pointer.

"This is our current position." The officer slapped the map with his pointer. A drop of sweat slid down the side of his face, clung to his jaw. "The Falcon is far enough out not to be encountered by fishing vessels from Apoquaque, yet close enough into the quadrant to pick up any anomalies above, from, or around Apoquaque." The droplet fell to his collar, coloring it gray.

"I understand things will happen very quickly," Graham said.

Francis didn't know whom he was addressing, where he was looking.

"That's been the pattern," Protsky answered.

"Timing is everything." Graham leaned back in his chair, his long, perfectly manicured fingers touching each other. "Everything," he said as if he was a man possessed of some profound spiritual knowledge. "Protsky, have you shown Dr. Chance the cylinder?"

"Not yet. We just—"

"Ah, Dr. Chance, I think you'll find it quite beautiful."

Francis didn't know what to say, or if he was even expected to say anything. He remained quiet.

Graham smiled as if he appreciated his silence, perhaps taking it as a mark of intelligence or cunning. "Gentlemen," Graham addressed the captain and his men. "We will need some time alone."

The captain stiffened, rose without speaking, walked out of the room, and followed one after the other by his men. The last man closed the door behind him.

"Protsky, Dr. Chance knows what we expect of him? What we can offer him in return?"

"I know you need my help in deciphering the glyphs." Francis decided to answer for himself but not to mention Morey, not yet. "You are allowing me access to an archeological treasure."

"Archeological treasure," Graham laughed softly. It was an odd laugh, like he had never learned how to laugh naturally. It was unnerving.

"Am I wrong?"

Graham moved back slightly. A reaction to being questioned?

"Dr. Chance, you are wrong on neither account." His elbows were on the arms of his chair, colorless fingertips touching one another. "There are two cylinders, possibly more. I possess one. Morey Chance, your daughter, has the other. Protsky has instructed you on the anomaly phenomena." Graham's head tilted slightly in Protsky's direction, Protsky nodded. "I believe the phenomena and the cylinder are inextricably linked, the glyphs the key." Graham fell silent, turned his pearl King cobra face in Francis's direction.

There was something oddly attractive about Graham. It wasn't his physical appearance. It had more to do with his authority. He hid nothing about his enjoyment of it. He exuded power. He sensed Graham was fishing for a worthy sparring partner. Francis did not know how much Graham knew - about the community, about those to whom the cylinders belonged. He needed to appear cooperative but be careful not to share too much. He knew the bottom line. To keep Morey alive, he must stay valuable.

"I've studied the glyphs," Francis offered, "they bear no resemblance to, nor do they seem to evolve from, any known ancient language. They are most probably unique to an undiscovered people and that is the reason they remain undecipherable." There was that feeling in his brain again. Stronger this time.

Graham remained quiet, still as the cobra before it strikes. The longer he said nothing, the more acute the feeling got. "Protsky," Graham broke his silence.

"Dr. Chance is correct. My computers have run correlations with every ancient language - Ethiopic, Sanskrit, Zend, Pahlevi, Arabic, Chaldean, Persian, Minoan - and modern dialects such as the Bushman, Aborigines, tribes found deep within the Amazon. We've found no match."

"An irresistible challenge," Graham's ivory chin rose, his voice had a dreamy quality. "I see what drew you to this, Dr. Chance. There is a touch of magic about unknown writing, and a corresponding glory is bound to attach itself to the person who first solves its mystery. Think of it," he leaned toward him. "Francis Chance, long considered the mad man of archeology, deciphers the glyphs of an ancient culture, an unknown ancient culture. Not only proves he was far from mad but guarantees himself a prominent place in the history books among the most renowned archeologists."

"You've forgotten one thing."

"And what is that?"

"I'm a dead man."

Graham did that laugh thing. "That can be changed. I've done such resurrections before." He paused, perhaps allowing his power to sink in. "I'm sure it won't surprise you that I've done a thorough check into your background. I know your genius quite well, and I know how fame deservedly yours has eluded you."

Francis did not want to respond to this carrot. "Protsky was quite explicit on the plane. I believe you know my motivation."

"Ah, Morey," Graham turned toward Protsky with a slight look of disdain. "Protsky has no finesse. Discourteous and tactless." Francis saw Protsky's fists clench. Graham's face turned back to him. "So you and I have different pots of gold at the end of the same rainbow. Yours is very noble indeed. Mine…well I'm sure you've figured out mine."

Francis felt himself losing patience. "Deciphering the glyphs may prove impossible. There were only four glyphs on the cylinder I studied. Unless your cylinder—"

"Four. And exactly the same."

Francis was stunned. They had seen Morey's cylinder, compared it with the one they had.

"So what's the problem? Is four not better than three?"

Francis guessed Graham was the kind of man who didn't tolerate obstacles. He expected solutions.

"I'm sure you know the story of the Rosetta stone," Francis said, "how it was eventually cracked." Graham remained stonily silent. Uncomfortably, he continued. "It's not the number of glyphs that's the problem. It's the fact that both cylinders have the same four glyphs. If we had different glyphs but one the same on each cylinder, we would have a constant. A constant is a starting place, a glyph that means the same thing. That's what makes constants so important. Often the constant is an important person's name. In the case of the Rosetta stone, it was Ramses. Every time the same character representing the R in Ramses is repeated you know what letter is being used. It's a starting point to cracking a language."

"And we have no constant."

"No constant. No starting point."

"So we must create our own." Graham responded almost cheerily. "A puzzle solved by a combination of logic and inspiration." He hummed "White Rabbit" by Jefferson Airplane, then broke off abruptly. "Would you like to see the cylinder?"

Francis felt his heart quicken. Then immediately he had that strange sensation in his brain as if someone else were in there. He saw himself reflected in Graham's dark lenses and sensed behind them Graham was looking into his very being.

"Yes," he said, then immediately felt sickened by the thought he was selling his soul to the devil.

29

"I don't understand," Morey cried in frustration.

"You don't understand anything." Hill's tone was stiff.

Morey was startled, a bit hurt. She looked down at the raft's floor.

"You don't understand your world. You merely manipulate it. You think there is something to realize, some place to get to, something to accomplish. You create this illusion that life is over there." Hill motioned out to sea with a sweep of her arm. "And you are over here." Her arm swung back, and she thrummed her hand twice on her chest. "You step away when life presents a problem, a dilemma, a pain. You move away to think about it from a safe distance, seeing life over there, while you are here."

"How am I to understand if I don't take a step back, look at it, figure it out?"

"Life is simpler." Hill's tone softened, as if she knew all this must be mind-boggling. "We see, hear, touch, taste, smell, think when we are in life. We are just that. We are life; we are not separate from it. The problem arises when we separate ourselves, withdraw from it, stand separate because we want to safely watch it, analyze it, control it. You must forget about understanding."

"But how can I learn the jump without understanding it?"

"To jump, you must not seek something outside of yourself. This is a very important point. I know you think you need to know more, to collect pieces of knowledge. Actually, that way you would end up not knowing anything at all. Instead of cluttering it with data, you must clear your mind. Empty it. If your mind is clear, understanding is already yours." Hill looked frustrated, as if she were trying to explain calculus to an infant. "You must be like a dark sky. Sometimes a flash of lightning will come through the dark sky. After it passes, there is nothing left but dark sky. The sky is never surprised at a thunderbolt. When lightening does flash, it's a wonderful sight. When we have emptiness, we are prepared for the flash. You should always live in the dark, empty sky. The sky is always the sky. Even though clouds and lightening come, the sky is not disturbed. Be the dark sky, and you will be able to jump without understanding, without intellectualizing, simply by intending to do it as you did with the cylinder. You intended it to open, and it did."

Morey looked out over the water. She tried to focus, but her head hurt. It was like Hill was speaking another language. Her thoughts drifted away, ran through all of the things that had happened since she stepped off the ferry. It felt like a lifetime ago. For days now, she rose every morning well before Katherine and spent each day out on the water with Hill and Maker, listening to Hill's lessons, trying to do this thing called the jump. Trying to understand the foreign things she spoke of. Hill had taught her that the human form presented itself as energy in the form of a luminous sphere. At the center of the sphere, about an inch above the navel was the centering vertex.

"Our way of perceiving the world changes when we learn to move the vertex," Hill had said. "In fact, when we dream wonderful, miraculous dreams, it is because our vertex has shifted. People who have dreams of premonition have displaced their vertex unknowingly, fixed it in a new position, enabling them to see things that will be. But these are small shifts. What I am teaching you is much greater. You must do it awake. You must sustain it. Your jump is to become one with your sea lion."

Lessons had begun the second day out. Even with the relative safety of scuba gear, Morey felt cautious at first. She'd never fully realized how large and powerful sea lions were. She was out of her element, alone with them in theirs.

Each meeting began the same. Once Morey was in the water, Maker popped her head out like a cork, muzzled Morey's face, and with a snorting sniff, signaled her kiss of recognition. Then she dove, made a playful loop around Morey's legs, surfaced, and swam on her back, inviting Morey to follow.

"Grab on! She's telling you to grab her fin!"

Morey grabbed Maker's hind flipper with both hands and enjoyed the ride of her life, diving, and rolling, back floating. She felt Maker's enormous strength, vitality, her gentle playfulness. She never took Morey down too far, stayed too long, or shot up too fast. She was always careful. They chased fish together, played with seaweed, popped air bubbles. When they floated serenely together, a wonderful transformation overcame Morey, a seeming transportation of consciousness to a place where stillness and movement were the same, where the present was eternal.

Morey had begun to hate her scuba gear. She wished she could rip out her regulator, dump the tanks, and swim free. She wished for the freedom with which Maker was born. She wanted to learn the jump.

"Breathe in the energy. Relax. Don't analyze. Observe. See what you can see out of the corner of your eye." Hill's words coaxed her. "You already have total access. You just have to trust it. You're a gifted flyer. You must learn the maneuver, a magical act thousands of years old that will free you for unimaginable flight. You must awaken your energy body. See the energy. Direct the energy out toward Maker. You must trust in your energy body completely. Learn to navigate it. Then, when you are ready, jump."

The same litany over and over, Morey's head throbbed with Hill's words.

"The first time will take all your courage," Hill's voice played like a mantra, "all your hope. You must have no expectations. Access your energy body. Pull your energy outside of you. Direct your energy, and jump into the void of pure perception."

Morey sat cross-legged on the raft with her eyes closed. She had listened intently to all Hill's words, had thought she understood their meaning. But she felt nowhere closer to doing this thing Hill called the jump.

"Damn it!" Morey opened her eyes, totally exasperated. "I just can't do this. I'll never be able to do this." She felt heavy with disappointment.

"Not in a million years." She fell silent for a moment, "Maybe if you show me?"

"This is not the way it's done," Hill said sternly. Then her eyes glazed, and she looked like she was far away, contemplating a dire puzzle. A satisfied smile grew on her face. "Maybe for you it has to be. Of course, you're right," Hill sounded pleased. "Your father's half must see it."

That's when Morey felt it. It was a feeling of complete and utter surprise. A small, unconscious but integral part of her had remained determinedly skeptical and had stopped her from truly believing in all this mystical stuff about jumping. But Hill was going to do it. She was going to jump. This stuff was for real.

Hill settled into a yoga position, legs crossed, hands cupped over her knees. She rolled her shoulders back once and closed her eyes.

To Morey's amazement a soft, sage-colored light began to throb around Hill. The light waxed into a luminous sphere from the center of which pulsed live, incandescent strands. Thin, wavy wisps gathered, wove rope-like around each other, pulsated outward then suddenly, this glowing life force sped toward Morey. Startled, she jumped back just barely saving herself from tumbling overboard. The light throbbed inches from her face, toying with her, waving gently like a leaf on an invisible air cushion. Done with its teasing, with the same mercurial speed, the light pulled back toward Hill. Hill's sense of humor, Morey thought, trying to regain her composure, a little peeved.

"Very funny," she said.

The strands pushed closer together, compressing tighter and tighter until they were a single beam of light. With one push, a radiant arc flowed from Hill's center, curved over the side of the raft, and disappeared into the water, leaving it tainted with a flush of colored light. Morey hung her head overboard and watched the light subdued by depth and distance travel swiftly through the water like a missile seeking its target. Where was she going? Hill's light traveled too far for her to track. She straightened up, looked back at Hill, who sat peacefully, as if asleep.

She stole this opportunity to study her, her every nuance, the sun coloring her hair, her hair shading her face. For Morey, Hill possessed an electric, physical presence, but as she watched her sitting idly on the raft, eyes closed, body completely relaxed, she realized Hill contained a deep stillness. How much of this adventure was a result of her desire to fulfill her quest, and how much was her desire to be with this woman?

Morey wondered what Hill thought of her. Overly self-conscious of her own desires, she never let their gazes meet long enough to see, to answer the question: did Hill feel even a glimmer of the infatuation, the draw she felt? Being alone with her now was intoxicating. She drew herself up on her knees, inched closer.

Suddenly to the right of the raft, a large sea lion rocketed out of the water. Morey knew instantly this was not one of the band of five. This was a stranger. Again the sea lion leaped out of the water, rotating his body with exquisite grace, like a spindle in midair. Then he plunged back into the sea. Dazzling spray shot up from the water, hung glistening in the air.

The sea quieted. She saw the sea lion's body slicing through the water, racing straight for the raft at a speed she had not thought possible. Erupting from the water, soaring over the raft, drenching her with huge sea-foam spheres, this large, brown, perfect missile shimmered over her.

"Show off!" Morey cheered, laughing as a rain of ocean droplets pebbled the raft.

Then the sea lion was gone. The sea calmed to an eerie stillness. She watched the water for Hill's light. There it was, heading back toward the raft, separated now from her ocean host and racing home. In no time, it reached the raft. A stream of lit water arched over the raft and back into Hill's core. Hill opened her eyes, smiled. Morey smiled back, blushed.

"See? Nothing to it," Hill's eyes glimmered with playfulness. "What did my energy colors look like to you?"

"Now that I think about it, you were a pale gray and smoky green, kind of a forest through the fog look."

"Good. That's me. You are a soft rose with a touch of yellow."

"You've seen me?"

"You've learned more, come closer than you think. All you lack is the confidence, courage, intent."

"Sounds like quite a lot."

"No, you are very close. Very close, Morey," she said with conviction. "You see, I am not really teaching you anything."

"Run that by me again."

"It's like this. You came into this world with your mother's genes. You came in with these abilities. They're innate. You therefore already know them. Yes?"

"I guess so."

"I can't really teach you something you already know. Correct?"

"Yeah."

"But I can help you remember this thing you already know but have forgotten."

Morey just looked at Hill.

"This is what Maker and I are doing. We are helping you remember. Do you understand?"

"Sure," Morey said with no conviction.

"I've been thinking that perhaps you've done this, maybe as a child. Then you dismissed it or changed the memory because it seemed too bizarre."

Morey thought for a moment. "There was this crow."

"Good. You flew with him?"

"Well…yes."

"Try to remember what it was like."

She thought for a moment. "I reached out my hand." She remembered it now, more vividly than ever before, her small hand reaching, stretching to touch him. So close, almost there. "Everything became so slow. Then it was like the sun came out from behind a cloud, blinding white light everywhere. I felt pulled by it, sucked up into it."

"Excellent. The white light is the tunnel of the jump. What happened next?" Hill's voice was tense with controlled excitement.

"I just...let myself go. Then I was traveling inside him, stroking crow wings, threading through tree limbs. I saw, heard, and sensed in every way what it was like to be him." She felt her body grow warm. She had bought into her father's denial, had turned the memory into a child's extravagant dream. Her brain seemed to catch fire with the memory. She remembered her sensation of aliveness, how awareness increased tenfold. Why had she not believed in such ecstasy?

"You were free from thoughts."

"Yes." She felt a sense of utter release.

"The crow is the crow. Not caught up in personal thoughts that divorce him from experiencing. For him, there is just life living itself. People have lost this sense because they let themselves be carried away by the garbage in their whirling minds. They don't have to do that. It is theirs if they just remember."

She felt the hot beam of Hill's attention on her. The message: *we are close.*

"But how do I remember?"

"You remember by having the courage to remember. You remember by trusting the truth. By having the intent, by making the commitment no matter how frightening. Courage. Trust. Intent. Commit."

"Courage. Trust. Intent. Commit," Morey said with resolution. She swung her head back determinedly, settled into a yoga position, and closed her eyes. She cleared her mind, focused on Hill's counsel, and repeated her words over and over, rhythmically, like a chant.

"You remember by having the courage to remember. You remember by trusting the truth, by having the intent, by making the commitment, no matter how frightening."

She thought she heard Hill's voice, coaching, trailing off, a distant hypnotic beacon.

"Direct your energy body toward Maker. Navigate. Trust your energy body. Courage. Trust. Intent. Commit." Over and over, then again. "Courage. Trust. Intent. Commit."

Free fall, white light all around. An ineffable, ambient light. Falling. Falling. Like parachuting. A door had opened, and a strong suck of wind took her.

No panic. She didn't want to grab, to hold on, to fight. Then she stopped falling, started at last to float. A peace that required no explanation, no understanding, enveloped her. A gentle overwhelming power. Familiar – ah - huge. Filling her till she thought she could hold no more. Yet all she wanted was more. Light poured in where her eyes might have been. Light hued with green. Her visual perception slowly grew distinct. She was underwater.

Sunlight poured into the sea like fingers from God. Voices became audible. The voices of sea lions. High-pitched, eerie trills that rose in intensity, trailed off like distant echoes, rose again.

She rose in an ocean-green channel of light, broke the silvery surface. Her tightly closed nostrils opened, and she breathed in the salty, moist air. Water droplets beaded her drooping whiskers. She was traveling with the same small group of sea lions, friends from birth, each of them born on Little Apoquaque Island, each waiting for the return of the males to the colony for breeding season.

She dove deep, and her body responded automatically. Her ears and V-shaped nostrils closed. Her heart slowed from more than a hundred and fifty beats per minute to fewer than ten. She used her long flippers for propulsion almost as a bird flies through the air. No friction in the water, although it felt heavier than air. Her body was perfectly shaped to glide, speed, slice through the water. She was incredibly strong, agile. Speed was easy to attain, turns and loops second nature. There was no gravity here. Chilled water surrounded and rushed over her naked body, yet she felt warm, comfortable. Her rear flippers acted as stabilizers for effortless navigation. She glided obliquely upward, rejoined her companions. Here, the sea was thick with life. Herring, rockfish, squid, and cod were her favorites.

No thoughts composed of words, only pictures, sights, sounds, intentions. The intent to curve right. The intent to play with a friend. The intent to chase a meal. Long whiskers, marvelously sensitive antennae, responded to the tiniest vibration, reacted to minute movements.

A sudden turbulence alerted her. She snapped up a squid. Soft, salty. Pleased with her delicious meal, she looped gracefully backward, completed a full circle, sculled around a friend. She swam with her friend for a while, closely, slowly. Rolling on their backs beneath a school of fish, they watched this amorphous, quick, silvery cloud. They had known each other, hunted and played together, since they were pups.

She languidly swam through the water. Tiny bubbles rolled off her body and broke as she passed. Her incredibly sensitive ears heard their pop and click as well as the echo reflected from the school of fish above and the rocks below. For her, the sea was full of sounds. Shrimp snapped and crackled. Some fish made rasping, grating noises. Her companions grunted, groaned, squealed, and trilled distinct messages. Sound waves traveled faster in water. She heard a friend from more than a mile away.

She glided surely and effortlessly up, broke the silvery-white boundary between water and air. She exhaled, took a big luscious gulp of air, and saw herself and Hill on the raft.

Then the white light was back, blinding, everywhere. She felt different. Heavier, denser.

She opened her eyes.

She was back on the raft.

Morey looked around her at Maker's sweet face bobbing in the water, at Hill on the raft a few feet from her. She looked down at her hands, moved one finger, another. She brought her hands to her face, held it. She was back.

"My God, I did it." Her words came out quietly, almost unemotionally. But then she threw her head back and laughed, screamed as loud as she could, "I jumped!" Then she yelled it again, and one more time for good measure. She stood, not caring that she was tilting the raft, thrust her arms into the air, yelled again, not in words this time, just a triumphant yell, then fell to her knees and took a deep breath. She was overcome by emotions so powerful, so exultant, and simultaneously so humbling, that no matter how long she lived, she would never forget her feelings at this incredible moment, or be able to adequately describe the intensity of them.

"It was wonderful, incredible, indescribable. I was one with her," she said softly, awe creeping into her voice. "The anticipation, the excitement at catching a squid, its succulent taste, the joy of play with a friend, slicing through the water...," she trailed off. She felt luminous.

Hill looked at her face as if she had not seen this kind of expression in a long, long time. She seemed totally moved by her.

"Hill, I *saw* everything. I wasn't blind."

"When you are one with Maker, she can see."

Morey's face felt wet. She brought her hand up to her cheek. Tears. Hot, salty, wonderful tears. "My God, it was miraculous." Her voice hushed. "Maker's so vibrant, strong, wild, in the present moment, nothing more. It felt boundless, filling, almost too much, yet I know I could never get enough."

Morey felt totally overcome. Drunk with it. Before she knew what she was doing, she reached out, held Hill's head in her hands, and gave her a kiss. A kiss of gratitude for the woman who helped this exquisite thing happen. She pulled away from Hill, still holding her head, her fingers laced in her hair. She felt the breath of her. Looking into Hill's eyes, so close, so strong this exquisite magnetic pull, she let herself fall toward her.

This time she kissed her differently. Full-mouthed. A warm, generous kiss. She closed her eyes, and something wonderful happened. She felt something soulful embrace them, take them somewhere she had never been. In this vast place, there was no distinction between them, no boundary. She felt as if she had known this woman forever.

She opened her eyes, and the world came flooding back. Immediately, she pulled away.

"I apologize. I, uh—"

"No, don't—"

"I was—"

"Don't apologize."

"Overcome." Morey felt mortified. "I didn't mean to get so personal about it."

"Nothing personal taken."

"Exactly, OK then."

Maker barked, then barked again.

Morey stumbled back, away from Hill.

"She wants to make sure you're OK," Hill said.

"Yes. Oh, yes."

"Jumping into an animal is a partnership. Maker must have courage too, the courage to accept you. It is a communion."

Morey bent over the raft's side, let her hand play in the water. Maker sensed the movement and swam to her. She placed her head under Morey's hand, pushed gently into it for a moment, then dove and swam a short distance from the raft where she broke water and barked at Morey.

Hill laughed. "You two surely are connected." She flickered a smile at Morey. Then her face changed. "But Morey, there are cautions to these new wonders you are experiencing."

"Cautions. What do you mean?" How could anything so extraordinary have a downside?

But Hill's jaw was set tight, the way Morey had seen her set it before, as if reflecting on something foreboding, something that tore at her soul.

"The currents of these abilities you are honing make their own claims, fill the imagination with possibilities. Unfamiliar and exciting sensations and emotions stir. Such knowing marks us." The words Hill chose seemed odd. They had an ancient quality, as if spoken by some foreigner from a strange place, another time. "We develop new ways of expressing life, but with this must come reflection—reflection merged with respect for the unexpected movements of the new freedom."

Morey looked out over the water. Her thoughts drifted. She did not want to hear anything bad about the jump.

"Morey."

Her name cut the air. She looked up at Hill. Hill steadied her gaze on her, conveying that it was paramount she heard what Hill was saying.

"I'm listening."

"There are dangers. There are tenets to the jump," Hill said. "Today you accomplished your first jump. It was wonderful. Safe as a jump could possibly be. First, you know and can trust Maker. That is the primary rule. Suppose you decided to jump into a sea gull, and he flew far out to sea with you. Do you think you could find your way back to the raft, to your own body?"

Morey shrugged her shoulders, let them slump. "I suppose it would be much harder."

"Some can. But they are the very experienced. The masters. You must always protect your body when you jump." Hill said these words as if they haunted her. "Suppose I was ignorant of what was happening, found you, thought you needed help, took you away. Suppose I was not trustworthy." Her face looked enormously pained.

Morey's mind flooded with an array of possible disasters.

"For some, there is an even greater danger in jumping." Hill continued.

Morey wanted to tell Hill to stop. "What could be worse than what you just described?"

"The threat that comes from within. You now know how magnificent the jump is, how miraculous it is to be one with a wild animal. It is pure experience. Like when we were first born, when we lived before the ego arose. There is just seeing, hearing, touching, tasting, sensing. There is no past, no future, just what is. The *is* becomes immense, with infinite intimacies. Experiencing this is so intoxicating a strong attachment arises. Sometimes, if the attachment grows too strong, a renunciation occurs."

Morey's head was swimming.

"Renunciation," Morey sounded as if she'd never heard the word before.

"A renunciation of your old life, your real life, a desire to stay in the jump longer and longer, perhaps forever. This renunciation can cause you to get lost and not find, or even wish to find, your way back." Hill's jaw set straight, her body went rigid, as if she could not extricate herself from her apocalyptic message and the feelings it evoked. "A true master is wary of this enticement and knows how long she can stay in the jump. But Morey," Hill held her gaze, "these fears should not stop you. Just remember these three rules. Jump only into an entity you know and trust. Make certain your body is safe. Never stay in the jump too long. Never," Hill's look was intense.

"Never," Morey repeated. She could not look at Hill any longer. She turned, looked again out to sea.

"So did I pass my test?" Morey asked.

"Your test hasn't begun."

30

In the small room behind the glass wall, Francis stared down at the cylinder. He found it incredibly beautiful - smooth, elegant, breathtaking. The light bounced off its polished surface making it difficult to look at for any length of time. He wondered if Graham had felt the awe he felt now. He knew that unlike Morey's cylinder, which was symbolic, this one was the real deal. This one possessed powers.

"Was it in such pristine condition when you found it?"

"She's just as we found her." Protsky stood at his side, too close as usual.

The cylinder was contained in a glass box, which sat on top of a column. Francis walked around it.

"The box is wired not only for security purposes," Protsky watched him, "but microchips read everything on this puppy. Temperature, electromagnetic waves, composition, barometric pressure - you name it. All transmitted to our computers."

"And?"

"Static. No changes, nothing out of the ordinary."

Francis looked around the room, bare except for the column and glass box. The room was well lit. Small security cameras with red, glowing eyes hung from every corner. One stared down from directly above the column.

"Room's wired for everything, too," Protsky responded to Francis's look around. "One light bulb goes out, one molecule changes, we'd know immediately."

Francis studied the glyphs. Four, the same four, exactly like Morey's.

"I'll take you to your work station now." Protsky moved to the glass door.

"I need to work here, near the cylinder."

"Not possible. No one's allowed to work in here."

"How do you expect me—?"

"You'll have everything you need and then some," his tone was adamant. "Follow me," Protsky opened the glass door, stood waiting for him. "Chance," Protsky said impatiently.

Francis walked past Protsky, through the doorway, and into the command center. Seven sailors maintained strict vigilance at their monitors. No one looked up.

"Your station," Protsky swept his arm toward a vacant station, its monitor larger than any in the room, "the computer with my correlation program. Sit down. I'll show you."

Francis walked over and sat down. He examined the screen, blank except for seven icons at the top. Protsky bent down over his shoulder, reached for the mouse. The smell of Protsky sickened him. He rolled his chair back suddenly, catching Protsky's left knee. Protsky winced, straightened up, and moved back. Francis thought he heard a snicker from somewhere in the room.

"Talk me through it," Francis placed his hand on the mouse.

"Hit the first icon, top left," Protsky's voice was cool. "That's the language program. Computer's programmed to run any language correlation you want."

He hit the icon and a window opened to a two-column alpha list. The left column listed all the modern-day languages, the right, the ancient languages. He clicked on Cypriot, a form of Greek script used between six hundred and two hundred BC. The screen filled with Cypriot characters.

"I've run every language, ancient and modern, against the glyphs," Protsky stated smugly. "None are related. Try one."

Francis ignored his suggestion, closed out, hit the second icon, further annoying Protsky, he was sure. A view of Apoquaque filled the screen. Moving the mouse, he toured the shoreline. Where, he wondered was Morey at this moment? Now that she had her cylinder, what had she discovered? Francis had spent his life keeping the cylinder from Morey, pushing her away. Now he wanted nothing more than to see her again, explain why. Where was Feuer?

"This is not the time to sightsee." Protsky's voice brought Francis back.

He closed out the screen, hit the third icon. Here he could read all the data Protsky had told him the microchips in the glass room were recording. He flew through them, noting none of them changed significantly. The fourth icon opened up to a picture of a cylinder. Morey's cylinder. His blood ran cold. He recognized Katherine's kitchen table. Any hope that they were keeping a safe distance from her died. He hoped it hadn't been Feuer who snapped the picture. He clicked again on the fourth icon, and then scanned through his own research copied from his office files.

"Nothing like a touch of home," Protsky snickered.

If he ever got out of this alive, the first thing he'd do would be land his best right hook smack on Protsky's bloated face. He opened the fifth icon to encyclopedias, reference books, nautical maps. The sixth opened to Protsky's massive correlation program, equipped with a calculus computer. Francis scanned it. It contained an enormous amount of data relating to the anomaly and the cylinder. He scrolled back to the first page. There was a left box and a right box, both empty, where Francis assumed he could type something into each, click on the word *search* below, and wait to see if the items had any relationship to one another.

"I'm sure I've left nothing out," Protsky stated, "still, nothing correlates."

The last icon opened to a live view inside the room where the cylinder was secured. Moving the mouse Francis could see the room from every angle. More importantly, by holding down the right click button, he could zero in on the cylinder. He played with the magnification until just the glyphs filled the screen.

"I'll leave you to your work. We will meet Graham in three hours."

When Francis didn't respond, Protsky turned and walked away.

From an angle, he could see the command center reflected in his screen. He watched Protsky move to the right side of the room, to four computer stations set apart from the rest. He paced back and forth behind them, breathing down the sailors' necks. One sailor got up from his chair. Protsky sat, his back to Francis. He was glad to be rid of him. He needed to think.

His mind raced. They expected him to crack the glyphs, had told him Morey's life depended on it. Yet by now, Morey must know about her heritage and must be becoming part of the community. If he could by any miracle crack the glyphs, certainly this would place the community in jeopardy and Morey with them. It seems no matter what he did, Morey was in danger. One thing was clear - he must convince them he was cooperating, buy time.

Cooperate, the word repeated in his mind. Then there was that strange sensation, and suddenly, a searing pain like his brain was cleaved in two. His hands rose to his head. Tears came to his eyes and his mind lost its ability to focus for a moment. Then the pain was gone. Left was an incredible concentration aimed like the crosshairs of a rifle's scope at one target, and an odd feeling of well-being.

Yes. Good. He must get down to work. What had Graham said? Logic and inspiration. Yes. That was it. Need to break the paradigms, think outside the box.

He felt heady and exhilarated, ready to launch into unchartered waters, wild habitats, beyond the edge of human thinking. Open the mind so far it touches empty space like the fingers of a blind person exploring falling snow. Visit the place where stones evaporate.

He split the screen in two. Keeping his view of the cylinder in the glass room visible on the left side, on the right side he opened the picture of Morey's cylinder. Each cylinder contained four glyphs, all exactly the same. What was their underlying thread? What was between the lines? What could he not quite see? He needed to slow the juggling of thoughts, zero in on one subtle idea.

What was their secret?

31

The sound of waves bounced off the jetty walls like the soft thumps of a pillow fight. Sounds were different now, each one unique, full, resonant. The raft's steering rod vibrated, slowly tickled the palm of Morey's hand. Hill sat up front, wind billowing through her shirt. Morey piloted the raft past the jetty and into open water. She no longer needed to rely on Hill to find the sea lions. What had once been vast open water was now as easy to read as a road map. Things had changed; she had changed. She liked her newfound competence.

She had learned many things. Humble things, hardly noticed before, had become huge. She could testify to another world's vibrations, another world's scents. The sounds of sea lion language were intelligible. Sea lion facial expressions and body language were now part of her vocabulary.

Each time Morey jumped she sensed Maker's embrace, knew Maker welcomed their communion and gladly opened herself to it. When she entered the white light of the jump and sped through its channel, she was directed by a pull she came to realize was Maker's energy welcoming her, guiding her in. Once joined, she felt Maker's joy. Maker wanted Morey to feel her power. Being joined with Maker was like being in the company of an eager child bursting to share her world with a friend. And Maker's wealth was great.

The most vivid moments for Morey were in movement - racing, slicing through the water at incredible speeds, gliding effortlessly upward like a helium balloon, breaking the surface and filling her lungs with wet, luscious air. These moments made her heady. Maker's favorite thing was floating with her head bobbing like a cork, using her flippers like arms to rotate and watch her world full circle.

Morey had given also. When she joined with Maker, Maker had sight.

Morey knew intimately the other members of Maker's band of five females, each Hill had named. Maker, the leader despite her handicap, was the most intelligent. Casey pretended aloofness to hide timidity. Koda, Maker's dearest companion, was the first to start any play. Dash was sweet, quiet, unequivocally the fastest. Sarah, the largest, had the handsomest set of whiskers.

Up ahead, Koda swam in playful loops. Casey and Sarah bobbed peacefully, heads tilted full back, pointed skyward, eyes closed in the warmth of the sun. Their sea lion faces came alive as the raft approached.

Hill had taught Morey about the breeding season. Maker must find a mate soon so she could give birth to a single pup in almost a year during late spring when seasonal upwelling promoted a rich food supply that mothers could more readily find when they had to leave their pups and set off on feeding trips. Pups were tended carefully, their mothers staying with them for six months to a year, until they were weaned. Then the pups gathered together, began playing in shallow water, learning to swim in Little Apoquaque's cobble coves and tide pools.

Morey cut the engine. Koda and Dash were still engaged in rough-and-tumble play, grabbing at each other's tails. Koda surfaced, slapped the water's surface with her flipper, signaling her challenge for the chase. She dove, and her exuberant playmate followed. One of the bobbing heads barked. Maker. She swam to within ten feet of the raft, waited. She knew the routine.

Hill secured a small anchor. She had told Morey today both of them would jump. With both of them jumping, there was no room for error. Absolutely none. Hill would be joining with Tenor, the male she had joined with earlier.

Morey smiled at the memory of the sea lion skyrocketing over the raft. She assumed her jump position - legs crossed, palms down over her knees.

"Shall I wait for you?" She hoped Hill would agree.

Hill looked out to sea where Tenor had made his first appearance. "No. Go ahead."

"But will I swim with you?"

"That will be up to Maker," Hill said, but when she turned to Morey, Morey caught a faint glow of pleasure on Hill's face. Hill looked into her eyes, held her gaze until she broke away. "Maker's waiting," Hill said.

The time it took Morey to jump had significantly lessened. She closed her eyes, brought herself to the necessary state - half-meditative, half-hypnotic.

She had learned to see the world differently, to watch the world move at a much slower speed. She listened to the sounds of the sea with all her attention. Gradually sounds slowed, distorted, like an old record played at crawling speed. She waited until she discerned patterns in the sounds, waited until the patterns stretched, until they no longer possessed characteristics natural to the human ear. She looked for the gaps between the sounds. Huge gaps. Holes big enough to jump into. Then she jumped.

The white-light ride lasted only a few seconds, and they were one. She felt the exquisite absence of gravity, tilted her head, and pointed her nose, glided in that direction. Air bubbles gurgled from her open mouth, breath held, no want for more.

A male swam in the distance, watching her, alert to her every move. She sensed something internal. It felt like tension. Sexual tension. She dove, and the male, stronger and faster than she, followed. Tenor. She curved sharply, swiftly to the left. He was still with her. Close to the sandy bottom, her tail kicked up loose white sand into an underwater cloud. Up over a small hill, weaving through a kelp forest, she swam more adroitly, faster than ever. He was still with her. They surfaced. She turned to watch him. That was his signal.

He wooed her in a display of agility and strength. He soared through the water, looped, circled around her. He snorted and bubbled and somersaulted backward. He sped straight to her sandy bottom, kicked up a magnificent sand cloud, and rocketed back up and out of the sea in a leap. He splashed and thrashed with enormous speed and power.

She watching him loop and porpoise across the water, her body curved, tense with excitement. He approached slowly, and they swam together, touching frequently, sensually. He held her with his huge, bear-like flippers. His poem, his rhythmic verse of movement complete, he swam away.

The others were watching. She swam through them, circled Koda, and shared her fulfillment. Koda joined her; they swam together in celebration.

Then the light was back.

Hill was already back from her jump when Morey opened her eyes. The first thing she saw was Hill's face. Hill gazed at her, and she knew what she was saying. She turned her face away for a moment, looked to the open water. She turned back and looked into Hill's green-gray eyes, telling Hill everything she needed to know.

Hill rose and knelt directly in front of Morey. This time it was Hill who kissed her.

Their love was slow, tender. When they were done, no words were spoken, no promises were made as they lay holding each other.

32

"Time to meet Graham."

Francis jumped. He couldn't believe three hours had passed. He blinked and rubbed his eyes. It felt as if the computer screen had been branded into his brain. For hours, he had sat hardly moving a muscle, every tendon tense, at attention, his gaze focused on the glyphs. He rose stiffly and followed Protsky into the captain's conference room.

Graham sat in the same seat at the head of the table, staring into his laptop, its glow reflecting off his dark lenses.

"So what have you learned?" Graham asked, clicking his laptop closed.

"I've run through all of Protsky's language correlations. They prove our glyphs are not remotely connected to any known language, ancient or modern."

"What else?"

"The cylinder is static. It experiences no changes in temperature, wave emission, anything relating to physical change or the phenomena."

"We know all this already," Protsky complained.

Graham touched two manicured fingertips lightly to his colorless lips. "Go on."

"I split the computer screen into two screens. One accessing the camera focused on your cylinder, the other the photo of my daughter's cylinder."

Protsky blew air out between his lips, rolled his eyes.

Graham ignored him. "And?"

"Four glyphs. Four glyphs exactly the same."

"And?"

"And nothing. I've been sitting staring at the split screens for the last hour."

Protsky laughed, low, sarcastic.

"Staring at the two screens," Graham repeated. He removed his two fingers from his lips, placed his piano hands in front of him on the table, sat motionless.

So now Graham knew. He was lost, useless to them. Another cylinder handed to him on a silver platter, and he stood before it like an incompetent.

"Having them meld into your subconscious." He heard Graham's voice, low, thoughtful. "The subconscious is the birthplace of inspiration." The white cobra's head, smooth and taut, tilted upward musing.

Protsky's face fell.

"I need to speak with Dr. Chance alone." Graham said.

Protsky's face flushed deep red. He looked wounded. "But—"

"Now," Graham's voice was harsh.

Francis looked down at the floor, felt Protsky whoosh past him. When he heard the door shut, he looked up at Graham. Graham motioned for him to sit. Francis chose the seat furthest from Graham and sat down.

For the first time, Francis studied Graham, all the while sensing Graham was allowing, even welcoming this close inspection. Disturbingly Graham mesmerized. It wasn't so much his color – ghost white, moon white, androgynous body with skin antique lace white, neck a stylus of chalk, face changing ivory, pearl as light played the contours of his skin taut skull – that was the disquieting characteristic. It was the absence of color that unsettled, gave Francis the sense that what remained after the slow washing out of color was a monster. Francis sensed Graham must have spent his whole life exposed but clearly not vulnerable, not lacking in protection. Graham masterfully turned his marble singularity into a camouflage, a paradoxical disguise, the blank page that harbors the snake's invisible poison ink, evocative, seductive, lethal.

"Don't you love what is muted, marginal," Graham broke the silence, "what exists in the shadows of human thought. Sometimes its invisibility is a blessing. You know this, don't you, Francis," he half-smiled. "It is here the imagination can mutate and mate, become a place of wild growth, a breeding ground, an experimental lab for the thought not fully formed to stretch, roll over, eat. Inspiration is a shy wild animal sitting on the edges of life who wishes to be coaxed, urged, evoked, seduced. Sublime is it not, Francis, this place between chaos and form? Stupid little people live in their convincing world, where the lines are sharply drawn in black and white, where God separated the light from the darkness. You and I, we know the lines were never there in the first place."

Graham reminded Francis of a beautiful flesh-eating pitcher plant. Who wouldn't be drawn in by its enticing promise of exploration and sweet inspiration, in through the trap door, in to the place of no escape where the pitcher plant consumes its meal?

"Ancient artifacts as beautiful as the cylinder, what is usually inscribed on them?" Graham asked.

"Often they were gifts to great rulers, their glyphs a testimony to loyalty or an announcement of a great event to celebrate his rule, proclaiming the ruler's greatness."

"Proclaiming the ruler's greatness," Graham repeated in a dreamy voice, then seemed to drift away.

"Do my glasses bother you?"

The question came from left field. It jarred Francis. "Why no, not at all," he lied. The truth was he wanted to rip them off Graham's face. Graham had the advantage. Francis felt naked in front of unseen, prying snake eyes.

"Light sensitive since birth, a genetic disorder that causes the pupil to misform in uterus in the early weeks."

This was more than Francis wanted to know.

"Ancient Nordic tribes believed it was a sign of the divine right to rule." Graham seemed pleased by this fact.

"Fascinating," he lied. "Does this have something to do with the cylinder?"

"I've been thinking." Graham's alabaster chin rose. "What if the glyphs represent a formula? A new E equals mc squared. Except instead of nuclear fission, the formula is the key to creating the doorway."

Francis test-drove the idea. "Possible."

Graham was quiet for a moment. "There's something about you I don't understand." His voice was silky smooth.

"Maybe you don't need to."

"But I do," Graham laughed darkly. "Your motivation, is it as simple as a father's love?"

His face felt hot. He did not answer.

A look of pleasure rose in Graham's face. "You have tried to crack these glyphs before. Worked tirelessly, consumed by our little puzzle. If you had cracked them, what would you have done?"

A well of anger rose in Francis. He did not like this pseudo-therapy session. Yet Graham had hit on something. Something he'd never allowed himself to think about. He remembered the time when nothing, nothing mattered but deciphering the glyphs. And if he had accomplished it, he truly didn't know what he'd have done next.

"You've suffered humiliation. Shame." Graham would not let this go. "Your reputation ruined, condemned to waste away in the catacombs of Braddard College. Poor old crazy Dr. Chance, when all along you were right. Crack the glyphs," Graham's voice rose like a preacher making a point from the pulpit. "Prove your condemners wrong. Right this injustice." He paused. "Don't you hate them?" His voice was a soft hiss. "The community, they call themselves. Isn't that the last thing you want, to protect them?"

"Expose them." Graham's voice was stronger. "Get even. Revenge is a much stronger motivator. Love is such a pathetic emotion."

The carnivorous plant was hunting, hungry to trap its next meal.

Francis felt as if something brittle were breaking inside of him. *Don't go there*, he told himself. He was afraid of what he'd find. Afraid Graham was right. That there was some bitter seed lying dormant in his subconscious. He needed to stop this. The sense Graham knew him better than he knew himself shook him.

"I don't see where this is getting us."

Graham leaned back into his chair, turned his porcelain white hands palm side up and held them in midair, his shoulders rose. "Just a little getting-to-know-you session." He turned his hands over, rested them on the table as if he were playing a piano, a slight smile turning up the corners of his mouth, and he began humming, "Getting to Know You" from *My Fair Lady*. Then he broke off and the pleasure drained from Graham's face. "How would you like to proceed?"

Proceed? Francis was at a loss. What if nothing takes form, nothing emerges, no brilliant white flash of Aha lights up the neural pathways of his brain. He'd gone over everything, everything he'd examined in the past, and all of the new data Protsky had entered.

"There's something missing that I need," he said. It was worth a try and he needed to stay in the game, fake confidence.

"Missing?" Graham feigned intrigue. "Name it."

"I need the file on where your cylinder was found."

"Classified."

"It's the only piece of information I don't have. It may hold the key."

"Work without it."

Francis rose, turned to go.

"You know, Dr. Chance—"

Francis looked at him over his shoulder.

"I've never had anyone leave without being told he was dismissed." Graham's voice was toying, a hint of menace.

Francis ignored this warning, turned back to the door and started to walk. He heard that laugh of Graham's, then the sound of something sliding across the table. He stopped, turned. On the table was a computer disc.

"Take it. It's what you want."

33

Morey rolled the Hogue merlot in her mouth, relishing its warm slide down her throat. As the wine settled in her stomach, it spread a blush of heat. She had kept her days with Hill secret. Even as her memory of today filled her with pleasant, sensual warmth, she remained quiet.

Amazingly, Katherine had not asked one question about Morey's doings. Sitting tonight in their hickory rockers on the porch, Morey felt great affection for this woman who appreciated a mystery and was not impatient about its unfolding. She felt lucky to have her in her life, yet she sensed her aunt knew a great deal more than she let on about things - about her mother, about her outings with Hill, perhaps even about Morey's future.

Interestingly, none of this mattered to Morey. What mattered was her aunt seemed to be willing to let events play themselves out, including Katherine's own role in them, whatever that might be. What mattered was Katherine was somehow part of her strange new world. And this made her feel safer.

Morey stretched her long legs against the porch railing, wiggled her naked toes in the cool night air. She yawned and said she was turning in. Katherine raised her arm, fluttered her fingers in a gesture of good night.

As she did each night, Morey proceeded into the kitchen, washed and dried her crystal wine glass, walked into the dining room and placed the glass in its spot in the china cabinet. When she closed its door, she felt a slight shivering, a disturbing little quiver pulse through the glass door. She looked in at the glasses, and her eyes widened. The glasses began to shimmer, then tinkle, then sing as if played by some invisible hand. The resonating vibration amplified, sending the ringing glasses dancing, crashing into one another like macabre, frenetic wind-up toys. A lightening-fork crack sliced through the glass of the door with a sharp snap. She catapulted backward, stunned, and tumbled into a dining room chair.

Then the rumbling began. A thundering from deep below the house surged to the surface in waves, held the china cabinet in its invisible grasp, shook it convulsively, smashing its contents.

Morey's chair, the dining room table, the house jolted like some freakishly out-of-control amusement park ride.

Herman's earthquake.

With an enormous effort, Morey pulled herself up out of her chair and watched it ghost dance away and then with a jerking spasm, smash to the floor. Swaggering, lurching from wall to wall, she made her way out of the dining room, through the central hall, and jettisoned herself out the porch door. Grabbing the back of Katherine's rocker, she felt the quaking cease.

Wide-eyed, Katherine turned and looked up at her. "What is it, Bucket? You came out of the house like a bat out of hell."

"What? You didn't feel that?"

"Feel what?"

Shaken, dumbfounded, Morey stared back at her aunt, heard her heart pounding in her ears.

"Wait just a minute."

She turned, walked back into the house, stopped in the central hallway for a moment, and looked around. The old grandfather clock stood solidly on the bare wood floor, its pendulum swinging slowly. Everything looked normal.

Impossible.

She stepped into the dining room, afraid the floorboards would jerk under her feet. She stood in front of the china cabinet, arms hanging limply at her side, and looked blankly at the intact crystal glasses, each in its proper spot. Nothing disturbed.

She heard Katherine's voice calling, asking if she was OK, if everything was all right.

"My mistake. Everything's fine," she called back weakly, staring in disbelief at the cabinet. Yep, everything was just peachy. No matter she was losing her mind. Perhaps her mother really had been insane. What if lunacy was her heritage? She looked at her trembling hands, brought them up to her face, and held her head as if it might explode. She wanted to scream. She took a deep breath, then another, told herself to calm down.

Calm down.

Then the reality of what had happened sliced through her as vividly as an Arctic wind, paralyzing her with fear. She reeled as if hit by a heavy blow. Of course. It was a vision of *what would be.* One of those precognitions Hill had talked about.

Herman's earthquake was coming.

34

I t was past four in the morning. Francis sat at the correlation computer, bleary. He was alone in the command center except for one sailor
on watch. The room was dark. Small spotlights shone above his and
the sailor's terminals. He looked over to the glass room. Fully lit, its
white light contained, the room glowed surreally like a luminous deep-
sea creature full of secrets. Some of its light washed weakly through the
glass walls into the command center and then dissipated, not reaching
the area where he sat. Heaven and hell. He reached for the can of Diet
Coke next to his computer, swallowed three times before coming up
for air. Warm, flat, it had been sitting there too long.

He had created a file of loose ends. Pieces of information, none
tied to one another, none Protsky had considered important enough
to enter. Each he had run through Protsky's correlation program, hoping to find some relationship between them. Anything to open a door,
unlock a theory. He hit nothing but dead ends.

He'd entered the disc Graham had given him, read through it.
Graham was right. There was not much left in the classified report of
the day they acquired the cylinder. Thick black lines consumed whole
paragraphs, obliterated pages. He typed in the only pertinent information remaining - the owner's name, Anchor, the date, July seventeenth,
the time, 0400 hours, the time zone, X-ray, and the latitude and longitude, 75° east by 23° south. He remembered Protsky had told him this was
ground zero of an anomaly and the place where the cylinder's owner had
met an unfortunate accident. Francis knew it was no accident.

He hit a key, let the program run, and leaned back into his chair,
hands behind his head, fingers laced together. There was something

comforting about working again. The left side of his screen was still opened to the camera's view of the cylinder, shiny like new, safe in its glass box. He closed his eyes, thought of the years he'd labored, consumed with cracking the glyphs. Thought of how close he'd come to going over the edge, the last words he'd written in his journal.

I fear my mind is no longer clear. The glyphs do not match my original sketch. Something has changed.

Poor muddled thoughts germinated by an exhausted mind.

He sat bolt upright in his chair.

"How do I get past videos of the cylinder?" he said to the sailor he knew only as Henry, who sat three computers away.

"Past videos?"

"You know, videos taken a week ago, months ago. These cameras must be storing tapes." His voice was rising. He couldn't help it. He clicked on an icon. It opened to a view of the cylinder in the glass room.

Henry rolled his desk chair over and looked at Francis's computer screen. "Just hit view. A column of dates will appear, and then hit the date you want." Henry's look showed concern. "Maybe, it's time for some shut-eye. You've been at this nonstop for—"

"I'm fine," Francis snapped. He hit view and a column of dates fell below the cursor. He picked the date of the anomaly of Hluhluwe-Umfolozi, South Africa, May seventh, the day the African named Mbokwe described beautiful lights in the sky. On the right side of the screen, he ran the video of the cylinder during that day. He magnified the image till the four glyphs filled the right screen. He looked from left to right and back again, from the glyphs recorded on the May seventh video to the glyphs of the cylinder in the glass room.

The same. Exactly the same.

He was staring at the fourth glyph on the old video image when he thought he saw something impossible, something happening at 0900. He reversed the video, waited. There it was again, a movement, ever so slight, like a shadow passed over the glyphs. He remembered Protsky's words: *This box is so wired that if one light bulb went out, we'd know it.*

"Check May seventh, 0900," he barked.

"OK." Henry shook his head. "I'm there."

"Anybody in the room?"

"Nope."

"Any change in the lighting in the room? A light bulb out, somebody dimming the lights, anything?"

"None. Lighting's at a constant level."

"Nothing's changed? *Nothing?*"

"Nothing, sir."

He ran the video backward again, increased the magnification, played it, and waited. There it was again, except this time the shadow passed over all four glyphs. He was certain of it. It simulated the way the light changed the appearance of things that possess depth. Like how sunlight could make a pond of water look deeper or shallower, depending on the sun's angle. The way water changes light and alters vision. If the light was not changing, the glyphs were changing. Not in length, width, or depth, but in the angle of depth, something so slight, the human eye would not notice or would be tricked into believing it was the light that changed. Who would think to measure something so peculiar?

No wonder the artifact was carbon-dated as a fake. It constantly renewed itself. When the glyphs changed, it became new again.

"You onto something?" Henry yawned, stretched.

That startled him. He had almost forgotten Henry was there.

"Just another dead end," Francis modulated his voice to sound disappointed. "So this column of dates is the dates of all past anomalies?"

"Each and every one."

He looked at the dates, picked April first, April Fool's Day, which somehow seemed appropriate. He clicked on it. The video came up. He watched and waited. My God, there it was. He did the same for another date. It happened again. It had all come together, the pattern was clear. The glyphs changed, like a sundial. No one had looked for the right key. Position in time.

He envisioned the glyphs exactly at their recorded depth of 0.03 centimeters. Then like a pencil point 0.03 centimeters long, the point entered a small opening then tilted, moved about on a piece of paper, stopped at certain points, made its mark. Positions on a circle. Positions in place and time. It wasn't a language. It was a map and a clock.

"Henry, I'd like a reading on something."

"You name it, sir."

"For the date of the last recorded anomaly."

"Got it."

"What's the measurement of the glyphs' angle of depth at the exact moment of the anomaly?"

"Angle of depth? You mean they don't cut straight down into the artifact?"

"No. They angle slightly," he attempted to sound matter of fact. "Just can't remember if it's ten degrees to the right, six to the left. I'm getting fuzzy-headed," he gave him a weary look.

"Sure," Henry smiled sympathetically, "angle of depth." He pumped at the keyboard. Francis saw a hologram of the cylinder appear on Henry's screen. "Seems each glyph's got a different angle, did you know that?" Henry asked.

"Yeah, sorry. I'll need a reading on all four of them. No, better yet, get me in to your program and I'll check it for myself."

"No problem," Henry hit some keys and Francis's computer screen opened to the artifact's hologram.

"Thanks." Francis ran through each hologram of each anomaly and measured the glyphs. He reopened the correlation program. A program had finished its run. NO MATCHES FOUND blinked at him. He stared at the two empty search boxes for a moment, and then entered all the new information. He hit SEARCH, leaned back in his chair, and prayed.

"Next shift, Henry," Francis heard the voice of a new sailor, the sound of him entering from the door across the room and behind them. He looked at his computer clock. It was five in the morning. In his screen's reflection, Francis saw Henry rise from his chair.

"Any action?" The new sailor looked at Francis then took Henry's vacant seat.

"Just dead ends," Francis answered. He heard the sound of Henry's footfalls, the door closing as he exited.

"Name's Sam. At your service, Dr. Chance."

Francis turned and immediately froze. Shock coursed through him, and for a split second, he lost all bearings. The sailor, Sam, now sitting where Henry had sat was - Rupert Cirrus. In the dim light, the sailor's face looked like Rupert, but how was this possible? Then something weird happened. Francis's eyes blurred, his vision became unfocused, watery. The sailor's face looked like it was morphing, changing. Francis felt like he was going to throw up. He was about to utter Rupert's name when the world came flooding back into clear focus. This guy wasn't Rupert. Definitely there was a resemblance, but no, not Rupert. How the hell could it be?

"You OK?" The sailor named Sam asked.

"Yeah, fine." Francis turned away, gripped the desk till his fingers hurt, till the nausea subsided. *They did something to me. The concoction they gave me altered my brain chemistry. This is like some kind of flashback.* He was overcome with thirst. "Need some liquid," he heard himself croak. He drained what remained of his Diet Coke, held the can upside down, and wiggled it at Sam.

"Very thirsty."

There was a long silence as if Sam were carefully considering his request.

"OK. Be right back with it," he heard Sam say, and then Sam left the room.

Francis stared at the computer screen. PROGRAM RUNNING flashed in yellow letters. It hurt his head to look at it. What had they done to him? That weird feeling inside his head, like something else lived inside of him. Had they hypnotized him? Placed some insidious program in the neurocircuitry of his brain?

The screen went black. Then solid red letters filled the screen. MATCH FOUND.

"Jesus," he exhaled.

35

Morey stood at the shore. There was no wind. No breeze off the water. Waves quietly lapped the shore.

The dogs knew. Their gait was heavy, slow, tails limp between their haunches.

She heard the raft's engine, Hill heading in. Hill waved at her, smiled. She could not smile back, could not shake the pervasive sadness, the hideous sense of doom that had settled into her being the night before, the night of the phantom earthquake.

Hill beached the raft, let her get in. They rode out past the waves without speaking. She knew Hill sensed a difference in her, was allowing her the time, the space to express it. About halfway to where they met the sea lions, Morey turned to face Hill and broke the silence.

"Remember when you were first teaching me to jump?" her voice was edgy. She tried to control it.

Hill nodded slowly.

"You taught me the human form is energy." Her hands felt cold, clammy, her stomach in knots. "At the center of our being is the centering vertex. When we learn to move it, we learn to jump." She needed to start at the beginning, take things step by step. It grounded her, kept her calm, at some distance from the hysterical being screaming inside her head. "You explained to me about dreaming," she continued, "how sometimes when we dream miraculous dreams, it is because our vertex has shifted while we sleep."

Hill nodded again.

"Sometimes it gets fixed in a new position, and we see things that will be. We see the future."

Hill dropped her gaze like she was having difficulty looking at her.

"Last night, I believe I had a waking dream. A premonition of what is to come. It happened without my trying to move my vertex. It just happened." Her voice was rising. In her mind, she saw the china cabinet convulsing, glasses splintering into silvery shards, heard the angry grumbling rising from the earth. "Herman was right," she swung her gaze back to Apoquaque. "There will be an earthquake," her words tumbled out faster. "We have to get Katherine off Apoquaque. We have to warn everyone. Ethel, Herman, Charlie. Everyone," she broke off, choking, her throat so thick with emotion. She loved Apoquaque. She would never consider leaving it now, not after the time she spent with Maker, with Hill. Apoquaque was her true home, her only home. Just the thought of Apoquaque's destruction was enough to almost destroy her.

Hill said nothing.

She ached for Hill to tell her it was just a dream, that they could go on spending their days together out on the water with Maker and the other sea lions. She wanted to hear that this was all her quest was about. But she knew from Hill's expression that would be a lie.

"We have to leave Apoquaque," her tone was heavy, her words slower. She felt shattered, like a person realizing defeat was inevitable.

"Morey, I won't leave Apoquaque," Hill said clearly, firmly.

"You don't understand what I saw," Morey's voice cracked. "I'm telling you, Apoquaque is in danger. Apoquaque is going to be hit by an earthquake. What Herman warned us about will happen. I saw it. My God, I felt it." She was frantic for Hill to grasp the seriousness of her vision.

"I believe you, Morey. I believe you," Hill's voice was filled with sadness, but it had a more disturbing quality, a hollowness. "I know the earthquake is coming. I know it will happen soon."

"You know." Morey felt her jaw set.

"Listen to me. Katherine will be OK. Apoquaque will be OK. The epicenter of the earthquake will be at the oceanic fault line, exactly where Herman predicted. The only ones in danger are out there." She motioned in the direction they were heading, the direction of the sea lions and Little Apoquaque.

Morey followed Hill's gesture across the green-blue waters to where the sea lions' heads were bobbing in the water. Her friends.

She looked back at Hill, long and hard. She grew angrier and angrier. Then she remembered the oil rig.

"Herman's theory," she glared at Hill, "there will be a major oil spill."

"Yes."

"Yes?" Morey yelled. "How can you know these things and *do nothing*? We have to talk to Saturn Oil. We have to get them to stop drilling. Turn this raft around, Hill." Morey started to stand. If Hill was not going to turn the raft around, she would.

"Morey," Hill extended her arm, and the motion stopped Morey. "Herman Bristol is a respected scientist who worked for Saturn Oil for years. They did not listen to him despite his scientific evidence. They will not listen to us. We cannot stop Saturn Oil from drilling any more than we can stop the earthquake from happening."

Morey slumped down in utter disbelief. This couldn't be happening. Something had to be done. She wanted to scream at Hill to change things, to make everything safe again.

Hill cut the engine, let the raft drift. Immediately Maker's head broke the surface, a rockfish between her dog-like teeth, one of her favorite meals. She had brought it as a gift for Morey. Maker tossed the fish high in the air. It landed with a fleshy thud on the raft's rubberized floor.

Morey watched Maker scull in contented circles, waiting for Morey to join her. Her anger melted into a hollow, empty pain, the most horrible hopelessness she had ever felt. She bent over the raft's side, and let her hand play in the water. Maker sensed the vibration, swam to Morey's hand, placed the top of her head under it, pushed into it gently, held the familiar touch for a moment and then turned and dove. She broke water again a short distance from the raft, barked for Morey to join her.

They will die, she thought.

"There has to be something we can do. Something," Morey's words came out in a strangled cry.

"There is an option," Hill's voice was low, flat.

"Then we must do it."

"It is very—"

"We have to—"

"very dangerous.

"We have to try."

"Dangerous for you, Morey."

She looked at Hill. "My test."

Hill turned from her, looked out at the sea lions. "We might not save the sea lions, and you could be lost with them."

Hill did not turn back to her. Morey knew she wanted her to say no to whatever this option was. She wished Hill would look at her. She wished she would see some hope in her eyes. But she did not.

Morey sat there looking back at Apoquaque, trying to think of all the other things that were important. Apoquaque would be all right. Aunt Katherine, the wolf dogs would be all right. She would be all right. *She.*

It's not just she anymore.

It was us.

The sea lions would be left out in it, out in the underwater earthquake, their world suffocated by oil, their food source destroyed. When they came up for air, their bodies would be covered in oil. She had been told stories - how their bodies could no longer retain heat, how when their temperatures dropped, they started building fluid in their lungs, got pneumonia. Even if they survived the earthquake, they would die a slow, awful death.

Morey couldn't allow that. She had gone past where that could be allowed, gone past where she could have lived with herself. She had gone into a place of *we, not I.*

"Whatever this option, this test is, I must try it."

"You are the daughter of one of our wisest leaders, a leader of great talent." Hill's head turned, and Morey caught the look in her eyes. Hill's were the eyes of someone caught in a painful, cruel dilemma. It rattled her. "She left her daughter a quest, a quest that is incredibly difficult, that requires the utmost skill, a quest that might prove impossible even for a master."

"I'm scared enough."

"There's more."

"More?" Morey was stunned. How could there be more?

"Remember the hieroglyphics - the inscription etched into the cylinder that housed your necklace?"

"Yes, of course."

"The translation is *Harobed.*"

"Go on."

"Harobed is well known among the community. It is an ancient fable. The animals complained to God that people were spoiling every place they lived. Even when they moved, people would follow. Nothing was left for them. So God said to them, 'I shall keep one place no human will occupy, and one day I will take you there. I shall call it *Harobed.*'" Hill fell silent.

"Go on."

"The legendary place God set aside, his covenant with the animals," Hill looked at Morey solemnly, "it exists."

"What?"she laughed, low.

"Harobed is a planet that revolves around one of the stars in the system we call the Pleiades. We have been transporting animals there. We open a doorway in the sky, and they are transported safely."

Morey just stared at Hill, stared at her without seeing her, just kind of lost somewhere, her mind frozen with the word *insane.*

She heard Maker's bark as if from some faraway place, a very different bark, and the word *remember* fused into her mind. Remember what?

"How many planets in this star system?" she heard herself ask. From where had this question come?

"Three."

She heard the music now. Whooshing, whirling sounds. Saw her mother's radiant face smiling down upon her in her crib. Saw the glowing orb, its three spinning revolving spheres.

Harobed.

Remember this moment. It is your anchor. It will provide for you.

Then without feeling anything particular, she found tears sliding from the corners of her eyes. An ancient feeling, so familiar as to be imperceptible, touched an underground lake of tears.

Relief.

Her whole life had been in preparation for this moment. She *knew* her mother. For the first time, she saw her face clearly. Her impatience, the restlessness of her heart, its yearning was finally quieted.

"When?" she asked.

"This morning at 9:24. We have time for one more practice jump."

Morey felt the most peculiar calmness. "Why wait for the earthquake?" She looked out to Maker. "Why not transport them now?"

"Because the animals must choose to go, they must choose to leave their home. They do not do this easily. They have only chosen to go when they knew their lives were in immediate danger, when their numbers had decreased so dramatically survival of their kind would eventually prove impossible."

"And my part in this?"

"When the earthquake starts, the door will open. The energy opening this doorway lights up the sky. Beautiful multicolored lights. The light is their beacon, the invitation. The animals see it, move toward it, not in the sense of motion, but of intention. Like the intention necessary to jump. Only then, through their acceptance, can they be transported."

"And Maker can see only when I am joined with her."

"Only if Maker can see the lights will she be able to accept them. Only if she accepts them will the others of her band follow."

"Otherwise they will be left behind," Morey finished the thought.

"They will be left behind," Hill confirmed.

"Then it's settled. I will jump just when the earthquake starts. Maker will see the lights. They will be saved."

"It's not so simple," Hill's voice sharpened. "You must execute your jump perfectly. There is no room for error. Small things prove fatal."

"Small things prove fatal." Morey didn't know why she repeated Hill's words.

"When Maker sees the light, you must be keenly aware of her feelings. You must sense the moment of her acceptance, her intention to join the light. At that moment, you will have succeeded in saving her and the others. They will be transported. At that precise moment, you must jump back. You will not survive the transport. It is not meant for you. It is critical you understand this. Once Maker has accepted the light, once you feel her intention to leave, you must jump back."

She saw the dead seriousness on Hill's face, heard the life-or-death tone in her voice. Only if she was willing to risk her own life would Maker and the others have a chance to survive. This was something even a master might not pull off. Yet she felt no hesitation, only a singularity of purpose to do this right, to do this perfectly, to use everything she had been taught to save Maker and her friends.

She watched Maker scull in the water, her dog-like face pointing up to catch the sun's warmth, unaware of the impending danger.

"So this is it. It comes today."

"Today," Hill said solemnly.

"Then let's get on with it. One more practice jump."

She positioned herself in lotus position, left foot on right thigh, right foot on left. She closed her eyes, concentrated on her breath moving in and out of her body like a swinging door, listened to the sounds of the sea. Slower, slower - immeasurably slow.

The last thing she whispered before she jumped was, "Swim with me, one last time."

Light all around, within and without. No time, no space, this journey to Maker. Then she was there with Maker once more, experiencing her beautiful world of senses, sounds, and sights. There was something different about Maker, an essence, a knowing she had not had before. It was wise and full and tender and strong, this knowledge she was pregnant.

She broke the surface, opened her nostrils, and filled her lungs. He was near. She sensed it, waited, and like a rocket, his body glimmering with spray, he shot out of the water, arched in the air, and knifed back into the sea. She dove gracefully, waited for him to join her.

He swam to her. He knew too.

They swam together, not to hunt, not to play, but to strengthen their bond. They swam closely, in unison, sometimes lightly touching, water rushing between their sleek bodies.

Right turns, left turns, as if their two minds were one, two wills one. Elegant speed, slow ballet turns, close together, soulful joy in their union.

Hill knew it was time. The light sped to her, enveloped her, and she was back on the raft. She opened her eyes, saw Morey directly across from her, sitting in her lotus position, eyes open, watching her.

"Thanks for the invitation." Hill smiled.

Hill uncrossed her legs and moved toward her until they were face to face. She kissed Morey softly and deeply. A kiss that would echo in Hill's memory for a lifetime.

36

Katherine was alone in the house. She looked out the kitchen window to the patch of grass by her garden. She did not believe in miracles, at least not without struggle first. She knew too well there were no victories without victims.

She left the kitchen, walked to the barn door. She stopped, pulled out a thick, heavy key from her overall pocket, turned it over, feeling its shape, its weight. She thought how long this journey had taken from that first day, the day of that phenomenal thunderstorm. The day Francis Chance had met the being who was to become Morey's mother. Their union had created a unique child who had grown into a woman of magic, a woman who now understood the truth about her mother and her heritage.

Katherine let out a long deep sigh. She had selfishly looked forward to Morey's return to Apoquaque. But the joy at the thought of their reunion had always been tainted by fear, fear of the danger Morey would face if she chose to help. And she had known Morey would choose no other path, no matter the risks. Katherine had admired Morey since she was a little girl, had tried during those long summers to nurture her admirable qualities. Morey's innate sense of wonder at the natural world, her openness to places beyond the five senses, her indomitable strength of character were what Katherine thought of now.

She remembered the last summer Morey had spent with her, that awful scene in the library. She had wanted so much to let Morey know about her powers, knowing how she felt different from other children, always the outsider. But Katherine had promised Francis his little girl would be allowed to grow up like other children. Other children like him. She would not reveal the truth, not while Morey was a child. She would never let her know it was she who had met her father that day, she who had given birth to this miraculous child. She agreed to live the lie of being her aunt, of seeing her daughter only during summers on Apoquaque.

That day in the library she had been overcome by her own stubborn desires, had wanted to show Morey the cylinder, let her hold it, maybe let her open it. Before anything happened, there was Francis in the doorway. Furious. She had broken her promise. She could not be trusted. He feared for Morey's safety. He ranted that Katherine had seduced him only to get a child. It was then he threatened her. Morey would not return to Apoquaque, and if Katherine tried to contact her, he would expose Katherine and her kind.

Then the package from Francis arrived. Inside was Morey's cylinder, and she knew Francis had released her from her promise.

Katherine looked up at the sky. It had the same unnatural hue of that long-ago morning before the thunderstorm had hit and changed their worlds forever.

The time was near.

She reached for the padlock on the barn door, held it in her palm. It was heavy and old, rust coloring each rivet. She put the key into the padlock, turned it, felt the padlock's inner mechanisms move. The lock fell open. She placed the padlock on the ground and with both hands slid the barn door open. Wood moaned against rusted metal. The smell of mildewed wood and hay billowed out, causing Katherine to momentarily close her eyes.

The interior was nothing out of the ordinary: a typical old barn, long out of use, needing paint here, a nail there. She walked over to a ladder that led to a small loft, climbed it up into a straw-filled chamber. Light shafted between damaged slats in the roof. She walked to where the roof pitched sharply, stopped beneath a latched sliding door that was part of the roof. She opened the latch, slid the door open. Full daylight poured in, illuminating the yellow reeds of hay. She stood for a moment examining the tinge of the sky, said a silent prayer, turned and bent to the loft's floor.

Pushing some straw aside, she uncovered a cylinder, a larger version of the one that contained Morey's necklace. The sunlight bounced off its smooth brilliant surface. Katherine raised a hand to shield her eyes. Should Morey survive her test, this cylinder would be hers.

Again she looked at the sky.

The time was now.

She stared hesitantly at the cylinder for a moment and then concentrated her intent. The cylinder came to life with a hum.

37

Francis was seated at his terminal, euphoric, exhausted. The night's lack of sleep was taking its toll. His body had suffered from the weeks he'd been kept on ice. He'd lost a good deal of strength, and now his exhaustion compromised the only weapon he had - his clear mind. Sam had been joined by the day watch, each sailor now busy at his station. He looked around the room. He didn't know when it had happened, but he noticed the door to the captain's conference room, Graham's room, was open.

He got up from his chair and almost stumbled. He'd been hunched over the computer for hours, barely moving, almost afraid to breathe. Afraid Sam would recognize he was cracking the glyphs, afraid if he took a deep breath, he would awake to find it a dream. He moved slowly to the open door and looked inside. Graham, laptop open, was seated in his chair at the end of the table, facing the door.

"Come in," Graham said.

Graham looked different this morning. Healthier. His face had the flushed look of the living. Francis walked to the conference table, stopped. He did not sit. Graham did not ask him to.

Although his mind was exhausted, it was sharp in a certain way. He doubted he could multiply the simplest of numbers, but he felt keenly aware the way an animal must feel when it smells danger in the air, grows aware that the smallest mistake can mean death. His senses told him something, something about the color red.

Movement. Protsky stepped out from the shadows behind him.

"Good morning, Chance." Protsky's voice was strained, and in his attempt to sound matter of fact, he sounded all the more malevolent.

Red. There was a glow of red in the room.

Graham's linen white hands moved from his lap, and he placed them on the table in front of his laptop. Suddenly, like his face they, too, were transfused with pink.

Then he saw it, transferred the meaning to his brain. A red light shone from the laptop screen, reflected off Graham's face, hands, tinted the room. The red light of MATCH FOUND.

They knew. Of course. Graham's laptop was networked into Francis's computer. How stupid of him not to have thought of that.

"We have a little timeline problem," Graham's voice was ice. His hands moved to his laptop, clicked it closed. The room grayed. Graham's pale lashes, his other worldlinesss, his world without pigment returned. "Protsky has informed me the electromagnetic fields around Apoquaque are shifting, spiking toward the anomaly. Today is—"

"I've got something to tell you," His words hurried, he told himself to slow down.

The faintest smile crossed Graham's lips, lingered. The ghost man, secretive, sly and hungry, intent on winning, watched him. He turned his head briefly in Protsky's direction, then back to Francis. Protsky moved like a petulant little boy.

"Today is the day," Graham finished, and then his smile faded. "You've found something?"

"As amazing as it sounds," Francis said, trying to think quickly, "the cylinder changes."

"Most amazing," Graham feigned surprise. Two fingers moved to his lips.

Then Francis felt that searing pain in his head. So intense he almost blacked out from it. *Cooperate.* There was no sense in lying now.

"I believe the cylinder is an extraordinary homing device," Francis heard himself say. "It sets the coordinates of the doorway. The first glyph gives the exact time of the opening," he took a breath, "the second, latitude and longitude, the third, the doorway's altitude." He stopped, stared at Graham's sunglasses, stunned he had given up so much. He was no more than their pathetic robot. "It's quite beautiful," he said softly.

"And the fourth?"

"My guess is that the fourth is the coordinates of the final destination." There was more movement than usual in the command center; he turned to look in. The atmosphere seemed tense, electric. He returned his gaze to Graham.

"Kind of like drawing a line in space and time from point A to point B," Graham sounded intrigued, rose from his chair. He had noticed the movement, too.

Francis realized he had never actually seen Graham standing. All arms and legs, spider-like, he did not move easily as if his body was on loan to him and he had never quite gotten used to it.

"The fourth glyph doesn't matter," Graham said coldly. He stood at the far end of the table, his face turned toward the open doorway.

"Doesn't matter? How could it not—"

"Nor does the first," Graham cut him off. "Protsky will deliver the time. Tell him."

Protsky stepped closer to him, close enough for Francis to read the arrogance on his face.

"I have programmed three computers." He emphasized the *I*. "Each fine-tuned to receive unique anomaly data. We know the peak of each anomaly, a peak that must be reached for the doorway to open. Each computer reacts when these levels are reached. My computers will tell us when the doorway has opened."

"Most important," Graham said, "Protsky's research tells us we have only a ninety-second window of time."

He turned to Protsky. Protsky picked up the narrative. "Once a computer receives the first spike of incoming data, the countdown begins. Each of the three computers must register certain anomaly levels. When all three do, the doorway is fully opened. This has never taken more than ninety seconds. Then the anomalies disappear, and the data returns to normal levels. We assume at this moment the doorway closes. From the beginning of the first anomaly data to the doorway closing, the time is always ninety seconds. No more. No less." Protsky's voice was firm.

"A ninety-second window," Graham emphasized. "Today is the day. Your job, Dr. Chance, is to deliver me latitude, longitude, and altitude."

"But—"

"The coordinates of the doorway. Precisely."

"It's not that simple."

"Make it simple." The menace in Graham's voice was clear, pointed, the game plan evident. He was in the power seat, ready to incinerate those who did not play by his rules.

"All I've fingered out is what the glyphs mean. To predict the coordinates of the doorway, I'd need to work out the equation. That's quite an undertaking. It's like saying we've decided why the apple falls from the tree - gravity. Now just hand me its equation."

"That's exactly what I'm saying." Graham's voice changed to something confident, matter-of-fact. "You've done amazingly well so far. Quite the ingenious mind. More than I ever hoped for. I was a bit worried that quirky little insanity thing might ring true." His attention shifted to the doorway to the command center, to the movement within. "This is your opportunity. Prove yourself not the laughing stock of archeology and save your daughter at the same time. As fond as I've grown of you," Graham paused, turned back to Francis, a thin smile on his alabaster face, "make no mistake, the equation is your collateral. Your life, your daughter's life, mean zero to me."

Francis said nothing.

Excited shouting came from the computer room. A sailor appeared at the door. "Sir, you are needed at command center. Missile's standing ready."

"A ninety-second window, Dr. Chance." Graham walked past Francis, Protsky following in his wake.

Francis grabbed Protsky's arm, stopped him. "Missile?

Protsky pulled his arm from Francis's grip. "A missile equipped with my own little homing device, the answer to the question of the fourth glyph - the final destination."

"But you know physics. Something the size of a missile would botch the successful transport of anything - anything living."

"Most probably. Glory has its sacrifices." Protsky turned, walked through the doorway into the command center.

What a complete fool he had been, thinking he could control any of this.

"What is it?" Francis heard Graham's voice. He moved so he could see him at the hub of the command center, surrounded by the semicircle of computer terminals.

"We're picking up some kind of electromagnetic signal from Apoquaque. It's being sent skyward." A sailor pointed to his screen.

"A signal? From where on Apoquaque?" Graham demanded.

"It's not coming from the town, sir. Best I can say is it's coming from the north sector of the island, mostly old farm houses and forest out there."

"Much as I suspected," Graham spoke contemptuously. "This could be the beginning."

Graham swung around to an officer standing at attention behind the left row of computers, the officer Francis had met before in the conference room, the one who had briefed Graham on the map.

"Missile standing ready," Graham commanded.

"Yes, sir," the officer responded.

"Protsky, get to your computers. Where's Chance?"

38

Morey sat at the raft's bow. She was feeling slightly nauseated, a feeling she was sure was brought on by nerves. Her mind raced, going over and over what she had to do, how to jump, how she couldn't miss the signals, couldn't miss Maker's intent to go into the light. Maker's life depended on her executing the jump perfectly. Perfectly. Maker had to see the light. Morey had to sense Maker's intention to move toward the light, join the light. Morey must sense this and get back out of the jump in time not to be carried away with Maker. Hill had told her this explicitly. Repeatedly. She had to jump back, or she would not survive.

Small things proved fatal.

Hill checked her laptop. She'd told Morey it would act as a seismograph, signal the beginning of the underwater earthquake.

Maker's face broke the water some distance from the raft. She barked her greeting.

"We're going to do this together," Morey said. "You and I, we're going to do this together."

Maker barked. A message Morey sensed was Maker's affirmation. Tears flooded Morey's eyes. As much as she understood that Maker had to undertake this journey to survive, she knew this was their good-bye. They had become two souls in union and when Maker left, part of Morey's soul would leave with her.

Morey looked at the sky. She had never seen such a strangely beautiful tinge in any sky before, yet something about its color was familiar, and she found this calming.

Hill's computer beeped.

"It's time," she announced simply.

Suddenly, Morey wanted to run into Hill's arms, hold her, tell her she loved her, how fearful she was she might never come back, never see her again. But instead something wonderful happened. She looked into Hill's eyes and for a brief moment was carried somewhere expansive, peaceful, safe. She sensed no matter what happened, it would be OK. It would be as it was meant to be. It would be perfect.

"I'm ready," she heard herself say, and she tumbled into the white tunnel of the jump.

At his terminal, Francis worked on the equation. The change in angle of the glyphs worked much like he expected. He needed to find the ratio that three-dimensionally correlated the change in angle to the Earth. This was not easy. He was acutely aware of Protsky who was too close, trying to see his work, an anxious schoolboy trying to cheat on the most important exam of his life.

"You'd better be ready when the doorway opens," Protsky snarled.

Francis ignored him. He felt Graham's gaze on him, burning into the back of his head. Graham was in full command, his smug, laid-back demeanor gone.

"Earthquake! Earthquake, sir!" shouted a sailor watching a computer screen of jumping seismograph lines.

"What the hell?" Graham said.

"Major earthquake, sir. Point nine on the Richter scale."

Francis looked over. Between Protsky and Graham, he saw the computer screen. At its center was a pulsating yellow dot sending concentric circles across what appeared to be a geologic map of the ocean floor.

"Protsky, what's this? Are earthquakes associated with the doorway?" Before Protsky could respond, a red light on Protsky's first computer station started flashing.

"Anomaly data coming in, sir," a sailor shouted.

Protsky hurried over, hunched over the computer, numbers and symbols streaming across its screen. "It's beginning," he said. "Start the countdown!"

"Yes, sir," A sailor hit a key on his computer pad.

In the top center of Francis's screen, the number ninety flashed, a second later, eighty-nine, then eighty-eight.

"Missile standing ready," Graham demanded.

"Standing ready, sir."

Protsky was in front of the remaining two computers. His babies. He had labored over them so no mistakes, no glitches would happen. But they were not responding.

"Eighty seconds, sir."

"Protsky, what's happening?" Graham's face turned to the blank screens of the two computers.

"I'm sure they're all working properly." Protsky pushed aside the sailor stationed at the second computer and punched furiously at the keys. He was sweating profusely.

"Seventy seconds, sir."

At that announcement, the red lights of the second computer began flashing.

"Station two alive," Protsky shouted relief in his voice.

"Sixty seconds, sir."

"Dr. Chance, we have less than sixty seconds to pinpoint the doorway and set our trajectory." Graham's voice was acid. "Protsky, where the hell is the third computer?"

Francis was looking at the glyphs on his screen in amazement, the shadow passing over them, changing them, as if God's arm waved over them. How beautiful it was. He followed the flux in angle, and his whole perspective changed.

"Fifty seconds, sir." Why, of course. Suddenly the pattern of it was clear to him, and he had to smile. It was pure. Fundamental. It took his breath away.

"Forty seconds, sir."

Francis's fingers sped over his computer's keys. All the while he worked his equation, he thought about how extraordinarily beautiful it was becoming. He believed he knew what Einstein felt when his equation gelled for the first time. He was absolutely heady.

He caught Protsky's reflection in his screen. Protsky hovered over the blank, lifeless third computer screen. The last link. The room smelled of his sweat.

"Thirty seconds, sir."

"Shit!" Protsky spat. "God damn it. Get out of the way." He swung his left arm full force into the sailor stationed at the blank screen and sent him crashing to the floor. He sat down and pounded at the keys.

"Twenty seconds."

At the nineteenth second, the last computer's red light went off.

"Doorway's fully open!" Protsky shouted.

The room went totally still.

Francis sensed Graham turning to him. "Dr. Chance, I—"

"Fifteen seconds, sir."

"—need those coordinates—"

"Fourteen."

"*now!*" Graham shouted.

Francis stared at the glyphs on his screen. No more shadow. He felt frozen in time. *Cooperate.*

"Thirteen seconds."

"Chance, the coordinates, now!"

Francis hit five keys on his keypad and sunk back in his chair. "Done," he announced.

Graham pivoted to the officer. "You receive that?"

"Yes, sir. Trajectory set, sir."

Underwater, joined with Maker, Morey sensed an incredible tenseness among the sea lion group, agitation caused by terror of the earthquake. They swam furiously around each other in elliptical circles, again and again, keeping their band tightly together. But they had no sense of where to go, what to do.

Then the lights came.

Heavenly fingers of rainbow colors filtered through the water, gracefully encircling, touching the group. There were little fingertips of electric impulses all over Maker's body. Pleasant. Quite wonderful. Morey was startled by a powerful emotion welling inside of her, definitely inside her, within her, yet it did not come from her. Gratitude. A message of love. From Maker to her. Maker thanking her. Maker saying good-bye.

"Good-bye, my dear friend," Morey messaged back. "You must go. Lead your group into the light. The light will protect you."

She felt Maker's intention, her acceptance of the fingers of light. The electricity grew more intense. Morey thought she heard the water hiss, then everything became absolutely quiet. A complete and total absence of sound. In its place was an overwhelming sense of safety, calm, togetherness. She floated effortlessly up with the other sea lions toward the surface into the center of the heavenly light. Every living being nearby joined them, rising with them. Starfish, sea eels, a multitude of fish, all ascending in the blissful light, it was happening. They were being transported.

I must jump. I must jump now.

Morey tried to hone in on the white tunnel. She could see it, but it was far away this time. Dim. Too much was going on, overpowering her. She was losing focus, beginning to feel faint, as if she were disappearing, vanishing.

She sensed the sea lion group stopping. Maker hesitated, sensed Morey's trouble and wanted to help. Morey knew she had no choice. She had to jump now no matter how distant, how dim the tunnel. Otherwise Maker would sacrifice herself to save Morey.

Morey felt a force sucking her into the transport. She pushed herself. Courage. Trust. Intent. Commit.

She jumped into the obscure gray tunnel.

"Ten seconds, sir."

"Launch!" Graham bellowed.

"Launch, sir."

"Eight seconds."

"She's up, sir!"

"Six."

"Five."

"Four."

"She's there! Exact position, sir!"

Tumultuous cheers swept through the control room, sailors high-fiving one another, slapping each other on the back, whooping and hollering. Francis remained at his computer, silent, exhausted.

"Congratulations, Dr. Chance." He heard Graham's voice behind him, close. He did not turn, did not respond. "Protsky worried," his voice was like silk, "I told him this artifact was part of you, pulsed in you as your own blood. Despite what you thought of us, you could not turn away from it."

Francis hated him.

"Sir, I'm getting a reading," a sailor announced.

"Good. The tracking device is working."

"Not exactly, sir. It's not that kind of reading."

"Damn it, be specific. What kind of reading?"

"It's the missile on radar, sir. She's still here."

"What do you mean, she's still here?"

"The missile, sir. She's still in our atmosphere. She's starting downward, pulled by gravity. She didn't enter the doorway, sir."

"But we set it for the doorway's coordinates?"

"Yes, sir. The coordinates Dr. Chance gave us from his computer."

Hill had watched the eerily beautiful panoply of colored lights undulate from the sky. Silent, fluid, radiant, the curtain had touched the surface of the sea. The sea had answered with a soft hiss. The lights had entered the water, spread like an atomic blast of luminescence until the entire ocean, as far as she could see, was alive with light. At that moment, she knew the lights were embracing all that was alive in the water, extending an invitation, a promise of new life. The doorway had opened.

Hill looked at Morey. Sitting Buddha-like on the raft, eyes closed, an enchanted sleeping peaceful child. Yet she was undertaking the most perilous journey of her life. Hill did not know if she would survive. She was down there risking everything for Maker and her companions. Hill admired Morey's courage, her reverence for Maker's world, her assumption of responsibility.

But it was far more than admiration she felt for her. Morey had opened something in her she'd long thought impenetrable. Since Anchor's death, she'd cultivated distance. Morey had melted the barriers. Hill had allowed Morey in, herself out, had become more than she had ever been.

Hill heard the hissing of the sea again, looked into the water and saw the light traveling up, floating toward the surface, leaving darker water behind. She checked the laptop, punched in the genetic code for Maker, Koda, Tenor. Nothing came back. Excellent. They were traveling within the light, protected. Good work, Morey.

Hill waited for her to awaken. What was taking her so long? She looked again at the water, all luminescence gone.

"Come on, Morey."

Hill watched Morey's immobile shape before her, waiting for endless seconds. None of this was happening. Not any of this. Except it was. She heard the hissing again, different this time. A strange kind of hissing she did not recognize. It sounded mechanical, a strange sound that came from the sky. Hill turned her head upward and saw a missile nose-diving earthward with incredible speed.

It slit the sea with the most enormous, ugly sound she'd ever heard. A huge, inverted funnel of seawater and spray rose hundreds of feet into the air and thundered back into the sea. Then there was nothing but eerie silence. Suddenly the raft dipped down, as if the sea beneath had disappeared, then a force sucked the raft back toward the missile's point of impact.

Dread gnawed at her. She looked wildly at Morey, tried shaking her, screamed at her to wake.

She heard it first. A surging sound alive with malevolence. She looked up and saw it moving toward them, a huge wall of water, building, speeding toward the raft.

She ran to the outboard motor and started it up. Their only hope was to outrun this thing. She kicked the throttle into high gear and sat down.

The thirty-foot wall of green water crashed over them, consumed the raft.

39

"Protsky," Graham's voice was ice. "Check Chance's work."

Francis stood, moved away from his computer. He watched Protsky pound the keys again and again, but nothing he did raised a single symbol. The screen remained blank, silent. He had deleted all his work.

Francis watched Graham's face swing toward the conference room door. Through the doorway, on the conference table, he would see his open laptop, black and lifeless, would know when he left him in the room alone, Francis had disengaged the network.

A hum, soft and beautiful, started in Francis's head. It was what he wanted. An honorable end. He'd never have allowed the cylinder to be used by these men. What would become of him, the hum calmly spoke. His eyes clouded over.

Protsky moved away from Francis's computer and started shouting. The hum grew louder. Francis sat back down, clicked on the glass room's icon, and brought up the cylinder's image. Beautiful.

The lights in the room flickered once but stayed on. He stiffened, finally allowing himself to hear the naked urgency in Protsky's tone. Sailors scrambled from their computer stations.

"The cylinder!" Graham cried.

Spiraling tendrils of white smoke rose like a toxic fog in the cylinder's room, climbed on quivering tentacles up its walls, across the ceiling, obscuring the room in white smoke that poured through the doorway into the command center. The beautiful hum emitted by the cylinder pressed on his eardrums.

A smoke detector bleated a shrill warning. The sharp scent of burning wires hit his nostrils, throat. Francis looked back at his computer screen. The glyphs were melting. The cylinder was destroying itself.

"Stop!" Graham's voice croaked. He grabbed at a sailor pushing past him.

The flat, ceaseless warning of the smoke alarm reverberated in Francis's head. Insistent, yet he did not move. His field of vision went fuzzy, opaque. Through the veil of white smoke, he made out the dim shape of Graham standing in the glass room, spider arms extended toward the glass box. A choking noise startled him, and for one awful moment, he thought Graham was laughing, then he saw how tightly Graham gripped the cylinder, and he watched as a wave rose through Graham's body, his body convulsed in racking horror.

"*My hands!*" Pain seared Graham's words.

Francis felt a man's grasp firm on his right elbow.

"Come with me, Dr. Chance." Through the white smoke, he made out Sam's face. "You did well. We're getting out of here."

40

Katherine heard the car grumbling along the gravel of her driveway. She had expected them.

Apoquaque Island was caught in a media frenzy. Helicopters swarmed overhead, carrying news crews that had come to chronicle another ecological disaster. The oil spill had swallowed Little Apoquaque. An oceanic earthquake had ruptured a Saturn Oil pipeline, the news reported, and although it was too soon to estimate the actual amount of crude oil that had escaped, Saturn Oil had issued a press release stating billions of gallons had been released before the leak was successfully plugged. Thankfully, a navy ship, the US Falcon, was within Apoquaque's waters when the earthquake hit and had been commandeered to head cleanup. So far the spill had been kept from Apoquaque Main.

"Katherine Chance, ma'am, would you please come to the door?" The voice was crisp, official.

"No need to," Katherine called from the garden.

She watched three men turn to face her.

Two stood by the front door. The third man was on the porch behind them, his hand resting on a rocker. There was something about the third man that made Katherine think he was not a member of the group, and she wondered why he was traveling with them.

"Excuse me, ma'am." One of the men by the front door took a step forward. "We're looking for Katherine Chance."

"You've found her." Katherine placed a hand on her forehead, shielding her eyes from the sun. She took a good look at the group. The two men were dressed in business suits, had short, military haircuts, looked in excellent physical shape. No more than thirty. In sharp contrast, the third man was hollow-eyed, unshaven, his greasy hair uncombed. He was older, short and overweight, and he had the disheveled, weary look of someone under stress. She knew what they wanted. With Anchor's cylinder destroyed, they needed another.

"We need to ask you some questions." The short, fat man rudely pushed his way to the front of the group.

"Questions? I'm afraid this is not a good day for questions."

"Not a good day?" the fat man smirked. "I know the feeling." He glanced bitterly at the other men on the porch. They did not look at him. He started to descend the porch steps.

"Wait right there," Katherine said. "I'm coming up." She threw down her gardening gloves and walked to the porch.

She climbed the porch steps, purposely walked past the pushy little fat man. She noticed he smelled strongly of sweat. She did her best to smile graciously at the young man who had spoken first. "I believe it's time for introductions."

"My apologies." He had a raised bruise on his right temple and the knuckles of his right hand were bandaged. "Name's Feuer, John Feuer. My partner here," he motioned to his clone, "is Charles Whiston. We are special agents of the NSA." He had blank eyes. Humorless. Cold. He took out his wallet and displayed his ID. "The other gentleman is Dr. Stanley Protsky."

She didn't know why, but she could not stop focusing on his bruise. He caught her staring.

"NSA?" she questioned.

"National Security Agency." His eyes betrayed something briefly, then quickly changed back to normal, but she caught the look, the look of someone who wanted to get even.

"The oil spill has brought the National Security Agency to our island?" she asked.

"Not exactly," Feuer's eyes narrowed slightly, and he smiled. At least his mouth did. The smile never caught his eyes. "We are on a rather tight schedule, Ms. Chance. So if I may ask you some questions, I promise to be as brief as possible."

"As I've said, today is not—"

"We're terribly sorry to hear about your niece, Morey Chance," Feuer's voice feigned sympathy. "We heard she was at sea with a scientist named Hill during the earthquake, that Hill managed to right their capsized raft and save herself, but your niece was swept away. We know every fishing boat on the island is out combing the waters for her. We want you to know the US Falcon has been added to the search for her."

"How very kind." She knew this man cared nothing about Morey's welfare. It was time to play mental chess. "Very well, I will do what I can to answer your questions, Mr. Feuer."

"How much can you tell me about this scientist, Hill?"

"Not much. Only that she was studying our island's ecosystem."

"Do you know Hill's full name? Where she's from?"

"I'm sorry, I don't."

"We knew Hill visited your home, dined with you," Feuer's tone hardened. "Yet you say you don't know her full name?"

His question froze her momentarily.

"Ms. Chance," he persisted, an edge of impatience to his voice.

"You might not understand this," she looked into his lifeless eyes, tried to find something. They were empty. "Our lifestyle on the island is very," she thought for a moment, "private. No need to ask someone her full name if she doesn't want to give it."

"I see," Feuer paused, "then you think she had something to hide?"

"I didn't say that."

"Do you have something to hide?"

"Certainly not."

"Then I don't suppose you mind if we look around the grounds."

"Be my guest."

"Whiston, take a look," his eyes flickered to Protsky, "take Protsky with you." Feuer flipped his hand, as if glad to be rid of him. Feuer remained apparently not done with Katherine.

She watched Whiston descend the porch steps and disappear around the side of the house, Protsky huffing behind him.

"And what was your niece's relationship to Hill?"

"My niece is a wildlife photographer," Katherine tried to sound as put-off as possible. "Hill is a scientist studying our local wildlife."

"Purely professional," Feuer's voice was snide.

Katherine did not respond.

"We are canvassing the houses in your part of the island. We visited the Dancers. Unfortunately, Charlie Dancer was not at home. His wife said he had gone out to sea to help with the rescue effort. We're here because the US Falcon picked up a peculiar signal coming from this sector of the island," Feuer shot Katherine a look, waited for her reply, when she did not respond, he continued, "a very strong signal, capable of traveling enormous distances."

Katherine stared back at him blankly.

"Don't suppose," Feuer continued, "you know of anything capable of sending such a signal?" He moved in closer, towering over her, an air of quiet menace about him.

"Well, no. Apoquaque doesn't even have a radio station. What could possibly send such a signal? Something very large, I imagine." Playing the naïve old lady was not one of her favorite roles, but it was her best card.

"Not necessarily," Feuer's voice was cold. He wasn't buying it.

"Nothing in the barn but old hay," Protsky said. He had returned his escort at his side. He lumbered up the porch steps, pulled out a handkerchief, and wiped the sweat from his face.

On the surface Feuer's manner didn't change, yet Katherine sensed him turn steely.

"I'm afraid I must ask you to come with me." Feuer signaled Whiston, and within seconds, Whiston's hand was tight on Katherine's elbow.

Katherine was about to protest when she noticed Feuer's gaze lock on the porch window. She turned in time to see the white lace curtains flutter back into place.

"Ethel, come on out of there," Katherine called.

Ethel blustered onto the porch, maneuvered past Whiston, and grasped Feuer's hand. Whiston looked confused, let go of Katherine's elbow, stepped aside.

"An agent of the NSA," Ethel said breathlessly, pumping Feuer's hand. "Ethel Bristol, editor of the *Apoquaque Free Press.*"

Feuer stiffened.

"Mr. Feuer is interested in some kind of signal the US Falcon picked up." Katherine stated.

"Oh my, sounds like front page. You simply can't go till I get an interview," Ethel purred.

"I don't give interviews," Feuer pulled his hand from Ethel's. His voice was strained.

Then Herman appeared at the porch door.

"You must forgive me," Katherine said to Feuer. "I should have mentioned I had company inside. This is Herman Bristol. I'm sure you've heard his name mentioned in connection with Saturn Oil, and perhaps you caught his interview last night on CNN."

Feuer said nothing. His gaze darted from Ethel to Herman, apparently sizing up the situation, deciding what to do.

Herman opened the screen door. Still Feuer stood there and said nothing. Katherine noticed Feuer's fists were clenched, the muscles of his jaw working hard. Whiston seemed frozen. She heard the fat man snickering quietly.

"Whiston, take Dr. Protsky to the car." Feuer turned to Katherine. "Ms. Chance," he said, his voice smooth, "considering the circumstances, I'm sure you'd rather be home waiting for news about your niece. My questions can wait. For now. Thank you for your time. I sincerely hope you hear good news." His voice was even but hard.

Feuer and his group headed down the driveway to their car. Feuer got in. Whiston guided Protsky to the back door, opened it, pushed him in, and then walked to the driver's door.

Before getting in, Whiston yelled to Katherine, "By the way, Ms. Chance, I'm afraid I surprised your two dogs out back. They went running into the woods. Thought you should know."

He got into the vehicle. They drove off.

Katherine waited till the car was out of sight, and then ran as fast as her legs could carry her to the back. She stopped at the barn by the old rain barrel where she could see the entire back grounds. She prayed she would see the dogs, prayed they would help her.

They were nowhere in sight.

She closed her eyes, stood stone-still. Listened. A breeze started somewhere. She heard it coming, rattling through the trees, louder and louder until it passed her like a breath of warm air, blowing her hair back, and pushing gently on her body. Then there was a calming heat, as though the sun had come out from behind a cloud and bathed her in its warm light. Eyes still closed, she sensed light illuminate the earth and felt as though a miraculous door was opening. The hair stood up on her arms as if suffused with static electricity. She felt something. She felt young again.

She opened her eyes slowly, waited till her vision adjusted to the brightness. Past her garden, at the very edge of the woods, sitting on their haunches were the two wolf-dogs. Directly behind them stood Morey.

41

Morey sat in the library in one of the two wingback chairs facing the fireplace, bundled in a blanket, shivering. She had never before felt so icy cold. Even her brain felt frozen.

Katherine stoked the fire, burning orange-yellow, growing in the fireplace. She stepped back, and Morey watched the fire consume the dry logs. Flames licked to the top of the hearth; heat spread into the room.

With tremendous effort, Morey willed herself to speak. "How did I get here?" The movement of her mouth, use of her voice caused a frigid blast to race up her spine. "What hap-pe-ned?" Her teeth chattered involuntarily.

Katherine turned to her and smiled a smile that could only be a mother's smile. "Hush, Bucket. All that matters is you're back."

"I know," Morey stammered. "I know you're my mother." Her eyes filled with tears, warm tears that felt wonderful.

Katherine walked over to her, wiped a tear from Morey's cheek with the back of her hand, and looked deeply into her eyes. "This is good."

"But why?"

"We knew your father had unearthed one of our cylinders at the site of a transport gone terribly wrong hundreds of years ago. The plan was simple. Get the cylinder back. I didn't count on his falling in love with me or me with him. Once he found out about the community, about me, he believed our love was a lie, that I had tricked him in order to retrieve the cylinder. By then, I was pregnant with you. You know he suffered when his reputation was ruined. And now he was reeling from learning that the woman he loved had - he thought - deceived him. Feeling manipulated, he despised me and the community. The more he learned of our powers, the more he realized your potential. Your father was so afraid for you. I understood why. Now you do too. For him, it became a battle against forces he feared might one day destroy you. Yet he promised to bring you to Apoquaque every summer, providing I kept your heritage a secret. I broke that promise that summer day in the library and any shred of trust between us dissolved. But his love for you won out. Remember, it was he who sent the cylinder back, he who returned your heritage to you."

Katherine walked to the other wingback chair and sat down. The two women sat in silence and watched the flames dance. The fire, hot and bright, threw trembling light into the farthest corners of the room. Its heat wrapped around Morey, flowed through her, and invaded her senses with the warmth of life. She, Hill on the raft, the beginning of the earthquake, Maker, the others going into the light, she remembered jumping into the obscure gray tunnel, and that was all she remembered.

There was no movement in the room except the wild dancing of the fire and the light it sent, light that washed up and down the room. Katherine faced the fire, did not turn to Morey as she began to speak. Morey closed her eyes.

You have been very brave, my daughter. Because of you, Maker and the sea lions are safe. You chose to join us, those with whom you share a bloodline. Believe in what your heart sees, what others can't see. We are those who can see in the dark.

Morey opened her eyes slowly, her gaze rose from the fire to the smoked-glass mirror. She saw her reflection and Katherine's there. She listened as Katherine continued.

Hill, Herman, Ethel, and many more are bound by the covenant to protect our animal brethren. To help them reach Harobed. Our depleted planet wobbles beneath man's weight. The environmental holocaust is underway, an event that has been accelerating for fifty thousand years, that will climax within a century if left unchecked. When today's babies reach sixty, half of the existing species will be extinct or endangered.

Morey listened to Katherine's words, watched their dark reflections in the mirror, saw their faces half in shadow, half in light.

For centuries we tried to teach the other humans of the planet. Some listened; some did great things. But we have a saying about them: Nothing learned; everything forgotten. They've lost the very feeling and idea of what a human being is.

Morey saw it then, fixed on it, but could not believe it. A knot formed in her stomach. *You're dreaming,* she thought. *You're dreaming and cannot wake up.*

Katherine turned her face to Morey. Morey looked at her.

What tiny changes in genes could have such enormous consequences? If it was the spoken word that raised Homo sapiens from the apes, then it was the unspoken word that kept Homo occultus safe.

Morey heard her, heard every word. But Katherine's lips were not moving.

You are not dreaming, Bucket. This is real. We have abilities other humans lack.. I knew you could hear me when you were on the porch the night of our dinner party. I did not speak aloud, yet I told you to use your mind to open the cylinder.

"In Africa, it was you who called my name."

Try it, Morey. Right now you can see that I am not speaking. Yet you hear me in your mind. Talk to me.

Where are Maker, Tenor, and the others?

They are safe. They have traveled to Harobed, a planet with healthy oceans.

Hill. What about Hill?

She is with Charlie, on Charlie's boat heading to one of our cloisters. What you didn't know, Morey, is that some people have been getting too close to learning about our existence. People who want to use our powers for evil purposes. Hill had to leave in order to protect herself. For now, they believe you may be just an unwitting photographer romantically linked to Hill. Ethel published your pictures in the Apoquaque Free Press. It helped promote the idea. The pictures turned out beautifully. First time Ethel did a color spread. Maker's face was front page. United Press picked it up. It made international papers. Ethel was very pleased. Herman has taken care of the computers in the cave, cleared their programs, left empty shells.

Hill. Will I see her again?

Katherine laughed. It was strange to hear her laugh in her mind. *Yes, your work with her is not done.*

Morey felt the knot in her stomach dissolve. *Is it just we who can speak this way because we are mother and daughter?*

All those of our bloodline can. We must direct our thoughts to those we wish to receive them. No one can hear our words unless we wish.

What am I to do with all of this?

Rest, get stronger. I can teach you now. I can teach you all of the things you missed learning as a child.

I'm not sure I understand all of this.

Morey heard Katherine's laugh again. It was warm, comforting.

All in good time, my daughter. If the universe has taught us anything, it is that reality is richer and more resourceful than our wildest dreams.

EPILOGUE

The two wolf-dogs sat on their haunches, their fur moved in the ocean's breath. Morey sat between them under a scrub pine tree overlooking the bluffs, the spot where Hill and she had started their journey. Under her mother's tutelage her abilities had grown and she sensed other potentials within, potentials that for now remained just outside her grasp.

The plague of oil had been contained but the sea lion rookery was destroyed. She found solace in the fact that because of the transport there was no loss of life, no suffering, no death. Most importantly, Maker was safe in her new home.

More government men had descended upon Apoquaque in search of the scientist known only as Hill. She knew Hill was far away by now and safe. She was proud of what they'd accomplished together and knew with certainty Hill would return.

A loud caw broke her thoughts. A black crow sat on a limb and looked down at her. Morey closed her eyes - then began to soar.

Made in the USA
Charleston, SC
21 July 2016